PRAISE FOR
ME AND THE ROBBERSONS

"With a deliciously anarchic Dahl-ish energy to it and
a lovely message to end, *ME AND THE ROBBERSONS*
is already a hit all over the world – it's about
time we got a chance to read it here"
Daniel Hahn, author and translator

"An absolute riot of a book, with a host of memorable
characters who you can't help but root for"
Simon Key, UK independent bookseller

"Witty, light and full of charm, this madcap
adventure will delight readers of all ages"
Florentyna Martin, Waterstones buyer

"*ME AND THE ROBBERSONS* is a brilliant,
topsy-turvy, humorous book full of surprising
twists and turns and sparkling with imagination"
Jury report, Silver Slate Pencil, The Netherlands

Dedicated to a Ford Transit 100 L 2.40

STRIPES PUBLISHING LIMITED
An imprint of the Little Tiger Group
1 Coda Studios, 189 Munster Road,
London SW6 6AW

www.littletiger.co.uk

Imported into the EEA by Penguin Random House Ireland,
Morrison Chambers, 32 Nassau Street, Dublin D02 YH68

Originally published in Finnish as *Me Rosvolat* by Otava, 2010

First published in Great Britain by Stripes Publishing Limited in 2021
Text copyright © Siri Kolu, 2010
English language translation © Ruth Urbom, 2021
Cover art © Tuuli Juusela, 2010
Published in the English language by arrangement with Rights & Brands

ISBN: 978-1-78895-317-7

This book has been selected to receive financial assistance from English PEN's "PEN Translates!"
programme, supported by Arts Council England. English PEN exists to promote literature and
our understanding of it, to uphold writers' freedoms around the world, to campaign against the
persecution and imprisonment of writers for stating their views, and to promote the friendly co-
operation of writers and the free exchange of ideas. www.englishpen.org

Supported using public funding by
**ARTS COUNCIL
ENGLAND**

This work has been published with the financial assistance of PEN... re Exchange

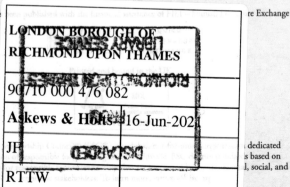

The Fores... dedicated
to the promot... s based on
agreed principle... l, social, and

WRITTEN BY SIRI KOLU

me
and the
Robbersons

TRANSLATED BY RUTH URBOM

LITTLE TIGER
LONDON

CHAPTER 1

in which we find out what a bandit van is like
and about Wild Karl's spur-of-the-moment hold-up

I was stolen during the second week in June – which was just as well, because this summer was turning out to be a joke. We were meant to go on a cycling trip, but then it started to drizzle, so we ended up staying at home. Then we were meant to go camping, but somebody landed my dad with some extra work, so that was cancelled too.

"It's nice for the whole family to do something together," Dad would always say when he was planning something, but he never asked us what we fancied doing. And his plans never came to anything. I had stopped believing in his promises of summer activities because of all the times they had been called off.

On that boiling hot day, the four of us were packed into Dad's new car on our way to visit Grandma. It was the most boring of all the summer's plans, at least as far as Primrose and I were concerned. The two of us were already in a foul mood and we were quarrelling in the back seat over a bag of pick 'n' mix sweets. As the older sister, Primrose always claimed the liquorice cars, even though she knew they were the only ones I wanted. But she just *had* to annoy me, the way she always did. That's what it was like in the car.

"Stop that racket back there right now, otherwise you're both going to be out of this car," Dad threatened.

Primrose stuck her tongue out at me. There was a liquorice car on it.

"That's right – you two listen to your father," Mum added, but nobody was listening. Mum didn't look at us. She had to keep her eyes on the road in front, otherwise she'd get travel-sick. "Maisie, you mustn't steal. It's rude and a nasty thing to do."

As usual, I got blamed for everything. Primrose always came out on top.

"Thief," said Primrose.

"Two-faced snitch," I said when nobody took my side.

We were totally unprepared for the attack when it came. We were just spending a summer's day arguing.

And then the bandit van struck.

Much later, after I'd been on many hold-ups, I could easily imagine what had been going on in the van…

The target – our car – was under careful observation

from behind a bend in the road. Then the van accelerated up to attack-speed. A pirate flag was hoisted on a mast through the sunroof and started to flap furiously. Hilda Robberson rounded the curve without braking. Of all the careless drivers in the world, Hilda was certainly the most reckless. She usually wore a bikini or a sleeveless top when she drove because she always steered with terrific force, causing her to work up a sweat.

The other Robbersons in the van were poised for action. Wild Karl, the chief bandit, was grasping one Flinger – a homemade metal bar that swung out of the van – ready to launch himself out of the vehicle, as his long braids flew in the wind. Golden Pete, a friend of the Robbersons, hung on to the other Flinger, practising his fierce robber grimace.

"I'm big enough to go robbing now too! I am!" Nine-year-old Charlie pestered. "I've already got this knife here."

"Oh, that's where the potato peeler got to," his mother Hilda said, keeping her eyes fixed on the road.

"If you were out there and had to say, 'Put your hands up', you'd probably start to cry," Hellie declared. Ignoring the van's mad speed, she carried on painting her toenails – each one a different colour. Hellie was twelve years old and super talented at everything, which made her the most dangerous bandit in the Robberson family. She was so wild she wasn't allowed to be a part of the hold-ups unless they wanted to cause real terror. Hellie sat in the back seat with her toes in the air, perfectly balanced, even though the van was skidding round as their bandit mum accelerated even more.

"Listen to yer dad now. He knows what's best," Golden Pete declared. His gold front teeth glinted as he tried to smile in Charlie's direction while still hanging on to his Flinger. To those who didn't know him, it would have looked less like a smile and more like a tiger baring its fangs. That is, a tiger with two golden teeth. "When yer dad says you're ready, you'll be ready."

"Yeah, right," said Charlie. "Probably some time after he's retired."

Wild Karl swung round on his Flinger, right up to Charlie's nose. "Listen here," he snarled. "I. Am. NEVERRR. Going. To. Retire. Say it!"

Charlie was frightened but laughing at the same time. "Erm… You. Are. NEVERRR. Going. To. Retire. Ever. OK, OK."

"I am sleek, fierce and sharp as steel!"

Hilda steered the bandit van into view of our BMW, then brought it to a stop in the middle of the road and started the countdown to launch. This countdown was vital to ensure that everybody would act at the same time. "Halt – check. Contact – check. Five–four–three–two… Flingers ready… Launch!"

During the countdown, the following things happened:

On 'Halt', the brakes squealed and the van jerked to a stop. On 'Contact', the front doors clattered open. Wild Karl and Golden Pete got a good foothold and focused on using the Flingers to propel themselves in front of the target vehicle in a single leap. They leaped at exactly the same time, on the 'Launch' command.

"Don't leave any witnesses," Hellie shouted as Wild Karl and Golden Pete hurled themselves into the best possible position for attack.

Which was right in front of us.

It was all over in a flash. Primrose thought she was on a reality TV show, and when Wild Karl grabbed the bag of sweets – and me – from the back seat, she actually sounded disappointed. "Hey, don't take Maisie!" she protested. "I'd be a much better competitor!"

I only had time to do one thing. As a big, hairy hand neared me, I seized my most treasured possession – my pink diary, which I never go anywhere without.

As there was no resistance during the hold-up, the bandits cleared out our car lightning fast. Dad was only worried about the car getting scratched and whether he might lose his no-claims bonus. It was only after the Robbersons' van had zoomed away that my parents realized I wasn't there any more.

"Well, well!" Wild Karl said with satisfaction once he'd swung back into the van with their loot.

Swinging on the Flinger had made my stomach churn. I've never liked amusement-park rides.

"Flingers inside – now!" Hilda ordered. "Doors – now!" There were two slams. "Gas – now!"

With screeching tyres, the bandit van left the scene. It was only when the van started off that it hit me – I was in the wrong vehicle, on my way to an unknown destination.

"Ahh… Liquorice cars, my fellow robbers," Golden Pete shouted as he chucked the pick 'n' mix bag on the back seat. "Somebody's got good taste in sweets."

"What have we got here?" Hellie asked, her eyes burning fiercely as she looked at me.

As they moved me into the back seat I clawed at them with my fingernails and yelled. Anybody who gets stolen ought to make some noise about it. But none of them took any notice. They were all going through the loot from the hold-up. Dad's cargo shorts were there, as well as his dog-eared copy of the *Guide to Finnish Wild Berries*. Mum's favourite bikini, which Hilda was modelling. Primrose's glittery nail varnish and her nail decorations, which Hellie declared to be useful and put in her locker. Mum's first-aid kit, containing everything from anti-itch cream to eye-wrinkle cream. Poor Mum, the mosquito bites would drive her mad without her anti-itch cream. I noticed they hadn't stolen much of mine. The only familiar thing I saw was my grey fleece hoodie, which was declared to be just right for Charlie.

"Hel-lo," I said, trying to attract their attention.

Only Charlie, who was around my age, looked at me with some curiosity. He put the hoodie down, as if he felt guilty about the stolen loot. I tried to look as if I didn't care.

"Hey, listen to me." My voice was a teeny-tiny crackle in my throat.

The van swerved some more as Hilda attempted to drive at full speed while looking back at us, rather than at the road.

"Karl. What. Is. That?" she asked in a tone that made the van feel colder than the inside of a fridge.

"What? What d'you mean?" Wild Karl tried to look innocent.

"That child. Explain! This instant!"

There was only one person fiercer than Hellie – Hilda when she lost her temper. And she was pretty close to losing it then.

"You're always saying I never make any quick decisions," Wild Karl said, sounding hurt. "You say I'm not a good problem-solver; that I need to take action. Trust my instinct. Well, now I've done it! For once I acted on the spur of the moment! I made an executive decision. And besides –" Wild Karl gave a secret grin to Charlie – "before we retire, all of us should be entitled to do some spur-of-the-moment hold-ups."

The van continued at breakneck speed. One minute we were still on the asphalt road that was familiar to me from our trips to Grandma's place, the next the van made a handbrake turn and raced off down a dirt track that I didn't know. What I *did* know was at that point we would have disappeared from Dad's sight – if he had even tried to follow us, that is. Now I was well and truly on my own in a van with this scary bunch.

"Well done," said Wild Karl.

I gave up watching the road behind us and looked around the van instead. There were two long seats in the back, facing each other. Between them was a small table, which was now leaning against the side of the van. The van was full of nooks and crannies, sagging storage bags and boxes under the seats, fold-up tables and mattresses on wheels hidden behind things. Yet everyone seemed to know exactly where everything was.

They chucked me on to the furthest seat at the back of the van, next to a window. I looked at the weird decorations in the windows: a whole row of Barbie dolls hanging by their necks, each one with a backcombed hairdo and a totally customized bandit look. Every single thing in the van seemed to emphasize how normal I was, and what a strange and hostile world I had been dragged into. I didn't dare to think what great danger I could be in.

"Perhaps we should…" Hilda began to say tentatively.

"We've got time to turn back…"

"We DEF-i-nite-ly should not," Wild Karl snapped. "End of discussion. We're not turning round. All spring I had to listen to you lot whingeing about how lonely you were. Well, here's a friend for you."

"But you're not allowed to steal friends," said Charlie. "That's not how it works."

I gave him a grateful look. If only he could get them to let me out of the van, I was sure I could find someone to help me.

"It's how it works right now," said Wild Karl. "That's the boss's rule."

To my disappointment, they all nodded and that was the end of the discussion. The Robbersons employed a robber chain of command. That was the first lesson I learned with them, and with that I gave up any hope of them letting me go.

On that long journey, I had plenty of time to observe the Robberson family. I wasn't tied up, and they hadn't put a blindfold on me like in the movies either. They didn't seem to be aware that they had brought a keen investigator into their midst. I observed Wild Karl's large, sweeping gestures; Hilda, who always seemed to be one step ahead of her husband – when Wild Karl flopped down on a chair after lunch, it had been placed there just a moment before. Golden Pete shuttled back and forth between the others as if he was the thread that held everything together: a tall, skinny thread with gold teeth, whose speech took me ages to figure out.

I observed the kids closest of all. Charlie, who tried to watch me secretly, and Hellie, who was dressed in camouflage clothing. She was the only one in the family who seemed to notice that I was observing them.

"Go ahead and look, it's free," Hellie said matter-of-factly. Not in a nasty way, just bluntly, which was a habit of hers. "But if I catch you taking notes, I'll read them."

She fixed me with a gaze the way a shark watches swimmers on the surface of the water.

Later that afternoon, the bandit van stopped at a peaceful spot near a lake, next to some trees. Hellie said she wanted to go for a swim to cool off. So that's what she did. We actually stopped our escape to go for a swim, as if we were normal people. Nobody thought to tie me up.

"You really ought to give me back. You'll get a good ransom," I said for at least the tenth time.

"Nope, we can't do that," Wild Karl said. He was rummaging around in an old holdall for some swimming trunks. "Huh, these have shrunk around the waist since last summer. I'll have to steal some new ones."

The others looked amused. Wild Karl was not a slim

man, and the trunks looked at least two sizes too small.

"Stealing, stealing," Hilda said, struggling to maintain a serious tone.

"But why can't you give me back?" I insisted.

Hellie raced into the water and began swimming front crawl perfectly, almost noiselessly.

"Giving back's not our thing," Wild Karl said. "Robbing's our thing. That's what we know how to do." He picked up a pair of scissors and cut the legs off an enormous pair of long johns. "Ta-daa! Swimming trunks!" Then he turned to me and said in a low tone, "Now you wouldn't AC-tually know this, but we've got a name to uphold. And with that reputation comes responsibility."

"It'll cause quite a buzz at the Summer Shindig when we rock up with a prisoner," added Golden Pete from his beach chair. "Folks will know for sure they've seen summat new," he said with a sigh of satisfaction. "It puts some feeling back in this business, ya know. We're doin' things by the book, old-school style. Like the Great Farnaby."

"Like the Great Farnaby," Wild Karl echoed. He was towelling himself off thoroughly, even though he had only dipped his toes in the water and promptly declared it far too cold for executive-level persons such as himself.

"You know, 'prisoner' is such a terribly dull word," Hilda said as she offered me a bag of pick 'n' mix. The bag that used to belong to Primrose and me. Then she leaned over to me in a motherly way. "Such a shame that there are hardly any liquorice cars left. You look like a liquorice sort of girl to me."

"Hijacked person," Wild Karl announced. He sat down and undid his braids. "We've got a huge advantage in having a hijacked person in our camp."

I sucked listlessly on a fruit bomb as I concentrated on their discussion. I wanted to retain every crumb of information that might help me to escape. I'd already made up my mind to make a run for it if that old man robber didn't agree to give me back. *So they've got some sort of summer festival*, I thought. That was good to know, even though I had no intention of being with them by then. The hustle and bustle of a big event would be the time to get away, if I hadn't managed it before.

Finally, I worked up the courage to ask, "Don't you want a big pile of money?"

But what would my stingy father actually be willing to pay if it came down to it? I bet not even half what he paid for his car. And they still had Primrose.

"What's that?" Wild Karl asked. He chomped into the last liquorice car, which really annoyed me. Although not getting to eat my favourite sweets felt surprisingly familiar.

Golden Pete burst out laughing. "Mouse farts, Karl, the kid's talking about mouse farts."

This conversation had taken a very strange turn.

"And what would we do with mouse farts, kid?" Wild Karl said, waving the half-eaten liquorice car in his hand. At least Primrose never did that. "What use are they?"

"Well, what sort of things do you want?" I asked, confused.

"What, do you want a list?" Hellie asked lazily as she shook water from her ear. She flopped down on an empty sun lounger and began leafing through a pop-music magazine she'd nicked from Primrose's bag.

"Why not?" I asked defiantly. I went to fetch my diary from the van, ignoring Hellie's sneering laughter about its pink flowery cover. I grabbed a pen from the dashboard and held it expectantly over the page until the Robbersons realized I was actually serious.

THE ROBBERSON FAMILY'S PREFERRED LOOT TO STEAL
Compiled by Maisie

1. pick 'n' mix, especially raspberry jellies (Hilda), chocolate (Karl), liquorice (Charlie), extremely strong liquorice (Pete, Karl, Hellie)
2. biscuits, especially ones with sugar on top or jam in the middle
3. meat (for Karl's robber roast)
4. mustard
5. other things to eat, especially new potatoes, strawberries

and other berries, homemade baked goods and sandwiches, pizza and other fast food
6. Barbie dolls (Hellie's collection)
7. reading material - books and magazines
8. full packs of playing cards (eight of spades missing from old one)
9. a decent fishing rod and reel
10. another camping tent to solve problems with sleeping arrangements

What they are looking for right now:

Croquet game (Charlie), small travel fridge and kettle that doesn't use much electricity (Hilda), fit boyfriend (Hellie)

"Nooo!" Hellie blurted. "Get rid of that last one. Charlie, you are soooo dead!"

Charlie cackled and ran away without looking where he was going, tripped over a tree root and went flying. I didn't need to watch sibling squabbles.

As soon as I had finished the list, it was snatched from my hands.

"This is good," said Hilda. "We'll keep this list at the front so the person who's riding shotgun can look at it just before our next hold-up."

"Verrry good," said Golden Pete.

The grown-ups were completely transfixed.

"You know, we've gone an entire year without an eight

of spades," Golden Pete continued. "Awful. We definitely ought to get those playing cards, innit."

My idea with the list had been to make it clear that I wasn't their ordinary loot, so they'd agree to return me to my family. Unfortunately things didn't go that way.

"One more thing," said Wild Karl.

"What's that, Boss?" Golden Pete piped up.

"This is good news for us, and bad news for you, girl," Wild Karl said as he placed his hands under his belly, as he always did when he was pleased about something. "Now there's no chance we'd let you go. You're the best bit of loot we've got from a hold-up in a long time. You're a smart kid."

CHAPTER 2

which is quite short, but long enough for Maisie to escape

The evening began to settle into night. We pitched camp next to a peaceful cove surrounded by woods. The Robbersons carried things from the van: sleeping bags, mats, tarpaulins. Golden Pete was busy trying to light the campfire, while Hilda placed some polystyrene cool boxes in a sheltered spot on the shore. Everyone swerved as they carried armfuls of stuff past me, as if I were a piece of furniture.

They haven't thought this through, I realized. *They don't know what to do with me.* That was precisely the moment I made up my mind that it was time to escape. I didn't plan it in any more detail than that. It didn't occur to me how incredibly stupid it was to run away late at night in an unfamiliar place. I thought I'd wait until the others were asleep and then sneak away from the camp. Then I'd find a main road, stop the nearest car and say, "Can I have a lift to the police station, please? I've been stolen." I imagined it would feel really satisfying to say that last bit out loud. Up to that point, the most exciting things in my life had been overnight camping trips with Guides and horse riding in the countryside. Nothing came close to the weird situation I was in now.

Soon I realized it was no use waiting for the bandits to go to sleep. The bright summer night began to dim, which meant it was nearly midnight, that brief moment of darkness before the sky would start to get lighter again. Everyone seemed totally alert and there was no mention of the children's bedtime. I decided to wait until they were all pottering around. I grabbed my diary, leaving our other stolen belongings behind, as I'd be able to move faster without carrying much. I began to creep towards the edge of camp.

I went towards the front of the van. A couple of steps in front of it. Then to the nearest tree. I paused behind the next tree. If anyone at the campsite thought to look for me, they wouldn't see me here. I moved from tree to tree, waiting until my pounding heart calmed down. Finally, I had left the glow of the campfire behind. I was surprised how dark the dirt road was with no light at all. I should have brought a torch with me.

"So where are we headed?" Hellie asked, shining a beam of torchlight around.

She was ten steps away and had obviously been following me the whole way. I don't know how I hadn't noticed. It was clear that even if I broke into a run, she'd be able to catch me. I'd seen her swim, so I knew I'd be no match for her.

"Is this going to be a long walk?" she asked.

"No, I just thought I'd look for some smaller branches for the campfire. It's hard to get the fire going," I blurted.

"Well," Hellie said, striding up to me. "You lie pretty well. And you're getting better at it all the time, prisoner. The boss got us an interesting new pet."

She aimed her torch at my face so I couldn't see the forest around me.

I decided to drop the act. "Let me go," I begged. "You've already got our stuff. I'm not going to be any use to you. Maybe you could just say I escaped and you couldn't catch me."

"Bad idea," Hellie said. She turned the torchlight away from me. "No one ever escapes from me – everybody knows that."

I knew I wasn't going to convince her. She nodded in the direction of camp, and I turned to walk back with her.

"Besides, you're wrong," she said, placing the torch under her chin the way people do when they tell ghost stories. "You're not useless. You're fun. And now you've tried to escape, you're even more fun. Let's make a deal." She leaped right up to me in one noiseless bound. "You don't try any more stunts like this, and I won't tell anyone about this little night-time excursion."

"If I say yes, you already know I'll be lying," I told her.

"Of course." Hellie grinned. "Looks like we both know how this story goes."

CHAPTER 3

in which we learn the basics of real robber cooking

I awoke to the smell of fried eggs. That told me instantly I wasn't at home. Mum only ever made hard-boiled eggs, which I hated peeling. Golden Pete was snoring next to me – Wild Karl had clearly put him on guard duty overnight. I wondered whether Hellie had told them about my attempt to escape. I concluded she hadn't.

I crawled out of the tent. The sun's rays pricked my sleepy eyes. I don't remember ever being outdoors so early.

"Morning, prisoner," Hellie said as she threw a knife at a target fixed to a pine tree.

"I'm no prisoner," I snapped.

"No name-calling, Hellie," Hilda said. "It makes people feel bad." Then she turned the eggs over just before they started to burn.

"Got a nasty mouth on yer, just like yer dad," Golden Pete told Hellie as he crawled out of the tent after me.

Hellie turned to me and said, "Yeah, sorry, prisoner." She retrieved the knife from the tree and threw another bullseye without even aiming. I understood I'd been very lucky last night. Instead of talking to me, Hellie could have just chucked a knife and pinned me to a tree trunk by my sleeve.

"Don't start, girls, not first thing in the morning," Hilda said to calm things down.

My desire to fight ebbed away when I saw Hilda slide the pan of fried eggs on to a plate. The picnic table was piled high with food. There were rye-bread sandwiches, which looked remarkably like my family's packed lunch from the day before. Meatballs and pickled gherkins. Slices of fried sausage. Mushrooms. A basket of little meat pasties. A huge stack of thin, round crispbreads. The chief of the bandit clan snapped a chunk as big as the side of the van off one crispbread and started piling it with all sorts of toppings. Apparently even a pasty could go on top of a crispbread if you were hungry enough.

"Come and eat, girl. Breakfast is the most important meal of the day. Isn't that right, Charlie?" Wild Karl said with a wink as he nudged his son in the ribs. Charlie was taking a big bite of his own pasty, which he'd piled with almost as many toppings as his dad had on his crispbread. The nudge gave Charlie a coughing fit. Wild Karl gave him a helpful thump on the back.

"Sausage warning!" Hellie announced, backing away. I also took a few steps back. The air was briefly filled with bits of sausage from Charlie's coughing.

"He does that every time we have sausage," Hellie explained. "Greedy piglet. You're not big enough for grown-up food."

"I'm not a piglet," Charlie protested.

"You're certainly no bandit," Hellie shot back.

I recalled my home and the silence round our breakfast table. I'd be sitting there, bored, while my parents each read their own newspaper and Primrose tapped out text messages and bopped along to music in her headphones as she ate. Nobody had anything to say to anyone else.

Once the quarrelling had died down, I seized my chance.

"That reminds me. When are you planning to take me home?" I enquired innocently.

"Would you like some eggs?" Hilda asked me. Without waiting for a reply, she piled a load of food on to a plate and plonked it down in front of me.

"Did you hear me?" I asked in reply.

Golden Pete stretched out his arm and before I knew it I had plopped down on to a folding chair.

"C'mon and eat now," he said. "Yer don't wanna be rude. Miss Hilda's eggs is world famous."

"Why will nobody listen to me?" I protested.

At least at home, my parents would respond to reason. Here, though, everyone just wolfed down their breakfast as if they hadn't even heard me. As if I were just a fly.

"Because in this family, we don't make any decisions before breakfast," Wild Karl growled. "That's why. Breakfast is the most important meal of the day."

"Dad hasn't had—" Charlie began.

"WHAT?" Wild Karl roared.

"I mean … the Bandit Chief Wild Karl does nothing until he's had his first mustard sandwich of the day."

Wild Karl had his hand and his mouth full of food, but he flexed his free arm and pounded his chest, Tarzan-style.

"That first sandwich is sacred," Hilda said before popping the top meatball from the meatball mountain into her mouth. "The only time we nearly got caught was the day we didn't have a proper breakfast."

"Don't ever speak of that!" Hellie shrieked and spat over her shoulder.

The entire family immediately stopped eating and spat over their shoulders. Then they resumed eating as if nothing had happened. I just stared.

"Come on, eat up your fried egg," Hilda told me. "We'll be leaving soon."

"What, with my hands?" I asked in horror. "Ugh, never!"

I was disgusted by the pickled gherkin trailing from the corner of Charlie's mouth and the lip-smacking sounds of

Wild Karl's chewing, but I was starting to feel faint from hunger. I looked around for a piece of kitchen paper. There was none. No loo roll either. Then I saw Golden Pete drinking straight from a bottle of mineral water he'd stolen from Mum and I realized I had no choice. I sighed, gingerly picked up a meat pasty with my fingertips and stuck two meatballs into it. After hesitating for a moment, I squeezed a stripe of mustard on top. I sat back in my chair, counted to three like you do when you're diving, and took a bite.

"Mmmmmm!" I said.

I couldn't control myself. I grabbed the mustard tube and squeezed some more on top, then added a couple of extra meatballs, though I was afraid it would seem greedy. When I saw Charlie had ten meatballs on top of his pasty, I decided I might as well eat the way bandits eat, at least today. I had never eaten anything so delicious.

"See? She was just hungry," Hilda said to Wild Karl. Then she turned to me. "Is it good?"

I nodded, but couldn't say anything with my mouth full. Golden Pete, Charlie and Wild Karl exchanged secretive nods.

"That's right," Hilda said. "You bet it's good. Hand-stolen and handmade."

"And hand-eaten," Hellie said. "What? You don't think we could steal cutlery if we wanted to?"

That made everyone laugh – even me, after a brief moment of embarrassment.

CHAPTER 4

in which there is a whole load of robbing

Over the next few days I learned everything there is to know about highway robbery. Things like how to spot a good target vehicle and how to 'sniff out' what it might be carrying, as Wild Karl put it. You could spot a car on its way to a summer cottage by the things packed in it. Sun hats, sleeping bags and badminton rackets in the rear window were a dead giveaway. Those were the cars it was worth following and robbing, because they had the most food: meat pasties and ready meals and crispbread.

I learned the difference between a frontal attack, a chase and an ambush. The chase was the preferred approach, where the bandits used binoculars to size up the vehicle in front. If it looked or felt like a good target for looting, they would start to sneak up from behind.

"You get the excitement of the hunt," Wild Karl said. "Lions chase antelope and bandit vans chase cars. It's the circle of life."

"And we get to give this girl a good workout," Hilda added, patting the van's dashboard.

They would stay on the car's tail until they reached a suitable stretch of road. At that point they would quickly overtake and swerve to a stop in front, blocking the car's path. There was an art to it: the distance had to be just enough for the target vehicle to brake and no more. A common rookie error was to block the road at a junction, leaving braver victims an opportunity to escape when they saw the pirate flag being hoisted through the van's sunroof.

"The most important thing for a highway bandit..." Wild Karl began with his eyes closed. Then he opened one eye a crack and continued, "How come you're not writing this down? This is valuable information."

KEY QUALITIES OF A GOOD HIGHWAY BANDIT
Recorded by Maisie

1) A good nose
Not everything is as it appears. A bandit won't succeed without a good nose. You use your nose to choose targets and to sniff out things like hidden goodies or police lurking in towns and cities.

"Without my nose, we wouldn't be here," Wild Karl said, pointing to his face. "Better clans than us have got caught just because their sense of smell was wonky."

"To help Karl's nose, we've also got an atlas," Hilda said. "We note down everything that might be useful later on. I record new things in it at almost every campsite."

"Let's move on," Wild Karl grumped. He was clearly annoyed by Hilda's interruption. But Hilda was driving the van, doing ninety kilometres an hour when the speed limit was sixty, so she couldn't really argue.

2) Looks

A bandit's credibility depends on their appearance. A politician has to look like a politician. A bandit has to look like a bandit. You can't leave any doubt in your target's mind as to whether it's a fancy-dress party or a hold-up. A sense of fear generates a desire to cooperate, which helps speed up the robbery process. That in turn reduces the chance of getting caught.

"Good teeth are particularly important," Wild Karl continued. Hellie and Charlie burst out laughing.

"Teeth?" I asked.

"We aim to look polite as our default expression, but from time to time you need to grimace a bit if you want to be taken seriously. The teeth are the key to this. Look at Golden Pete, and you'll see what I mean."

"Memorable choppers," Golden Pete said. "How's this for a grin, eh?"

3) Reputation

Creating and maintaining their reputation is of supreme importance to a highway robber. Your reputation should generate respect and fear, which are necessary for bandits to do their job. Reputations are earned by doing lots of daring robberies and winning police chases, if you get into any. Bandits meet up and compare reputations at the Summer Shindig, where they review the highlights of the year.

"And fight," Hilda said.

"Yes, yes, and fight," Wild Karl said, irritated. "But we also compare our reputations and glory."

"The fights are still the best, though," Charlie interjected.

A reputation can also be acquired by coming up with your own signature crime. A signature crime is a clever new method of robbery that employs particular creativity and daring.

"The Great Farnaby was in a class of his own there," Wild Karl recalled. "He took the whole profession to new heights. Without Farnaby, we'd still be lurking in the bushes with pistols."

"Farnaby," Golden Pete sighed in agreement. "A true classic.

That man showed us young folk how it's done, innit."

"Aaargh!" Hellie burst out. "This is so boring! Nobody would want to become a bandit based on that list. And being a bandit is the best thing there is. A nose, a reputation and looks. What do those have to do with any of this? They could just as well apply to any politician or office drone."

"A what?" I tried to ask, but didn't get a reply as the discussion grew more heated.

"I was thinking in order of importance," Wild Karl said. "Nose, reputation, looks – that's definitely the right order. No changing the list."

"Excuse me!" Hellie said.

"Very well," Wild Karl said. "At the request of Hellie Robberson…"

4) Attack skills
Attack skills include stopping cars, entering target vehicles, making threats and efficient getaways after a robbery.

5) Fitness
Robbery is a demanding job that involves working quickly under pressure. This requires—

"Oh, so you're in good shape, are you?" Hilda laughed, looking at Wild Karl's round belly.

"For my age, indeed I am," Wild Karl said. "You also

29

need to look after your nose and your reputation, and mine are in tip-top condition."

Hilda just gave Wild Karl a strangely affectionate look.

"All right, we'll add persistence later on." Wild Karl said. "For now add:"

This requires the bandit to possess excellent fitness as well as mental and emotional strength, even when conditions are not optimal.

6) Acting ability

Frontal attacks call for acting ability. In these attacks, the bandit van is parked on the opposite side of the road to the target vehicle to ask for directions or something similar. When the window or door of the target vehicle is opened, the robbery process begins. Good acting ability allows a bandit to override Item 2 (Looks) and adopt the appearance of an ordinary holidaymaker. Approachable. And then once the other car has stopped, the bandit can spring into action.

"That's the reason we rarely do frontal attacks," Hellie explained. "SOOO boring! Why would anybody want to look like a civilian, even for a moment?"

7) Persuasion

This includes all the ways of persuading people to give up

their belongings and cooperate during the loading process. Blackmail, threats, pressure, emphasizing their best interests, a bit of humour.

What was humorous about stealing me? I wondered. Maybe Mum and Dad's shocked expressions seemed funny when Wild Karl opened the back door and picked me up under one arm like a handbag. Then I remembered the confusion when I was brought into the bandit van. They didn't know what to do with me. Even though they're a bandit family, they'd never done anything like this. For some reason that thought made me feel a bit better.

8) Risk assessment

There are no easy targets. Each target comes with its own unique risks that must be analyzed. Where is the nearest police station? Are there any nosy neighbours who could be eyewitnesses? How will the passengers in the car behave? Will anyone try to defend themselves?

"Do you remember that lady back in March who waved her umbrella about?" Charlie asked. "We were all terrified here in the van, but fortunately Golden Pete handled her beautifully."

"Put her in the boot, didn't he," Hellie said.

"Yep, then we drove to the nearest shop and told 'em

there was an old dear stuck in her own car," Golden Pete said. "Not many folks know we've got such a big heart, innit."

9) Persistence

For the most part, robbing involves waiting around, although people don't usually talk about that. We wait for the right car and the right place to overtake. And we wait for the worst of the muddy season to be over, so we can drive on dirt roads again. Without persistence, a bandit would only last two weeks in the job at most.

"Winter," Hilda said, appearing to shiver in her sleeveless top. "Sometime, when we've set up camp in a good spot and haven't got anything else to do, one of us will tell you some horror stories about winter."

10) Stubbornness and initiative

Robbing is the act of transferring excess property from a target to yourself. If a bandit isn't stubborn, this is impossible to achieve.

"Boss, that's cheating," Hellie said. "You've got two qualities in one item. Those should be numbers ten and eleven."

"Now take Hellie here," Wild Karl said proudly. "No matter what I say, she never takes a bit of notice. She's going to make a first-rate bandit chief when she grows up."

I saw Hellie smiling her usual shark-like smile, but I also

saw Charlie's shoulders slump. Hilda had to nudge Wild Karl twice in the ribs before he thought to add, "Ah yes, and Charlie. He's going to become a gentleman robber any day now. He's got real heart and style."

Charlie gave a secret little grin at that.

Once we'd been through the theory, it was time for practice. Over the next two days, we robbed five cars so I could see what was really involved. I watched as a little Fiat was almost run into a ditch and then raided. The resulting haul was six huge tenderized steaks, fresh strawberries and the latest issue of *National Geographic* magazine for Wild Karl. I observed the threatening gestures needed to get the rear doors of a Toyota van open. That's usually where the cool boxes were. The loot: two new camping mattresses, swimming fins, ice lollies and a pack of cards, much to the delight of Golden Pete. I saw a new Nissan Primera practically run off the road because the driver was so frightened. That one got us two chocolate bars and some sun cream for Hilda. I witnessed a hold-up of a people carrier where Golden Pete had to climb up and sit on the bonnet to stop the dad losing his cool. Results: two new Barbie dolls and a video game. I saw an example of a frontal attack and how the driver of a shiny new Citroën – a grumpy middle-aged woman – was persuaded to lower her power-operated window and ask, "Well, what is it now?" Slim pickings that time: peas, a cucumber and some fish. Diet food is really no use to bandits.

After five cars I knew what to expect. I knew to hold on to the seat just before Hilda stepped on the gas. I could also recite the steps along with her:

"Halt – check. Contact – check. Five–four–three–two… Flingers ready… Launch!"

Then the van rocked as Golden Pete and Wild Karl swung out on either side. Another robbery was under way.

Sometimes it occurred to me that Wild Karl Robberson had chosen to educate me in the bandits' ways so that I would admire them. In between robberies we had long, heated discussions about which makes of car were the best targets to rob. Everyone tried to get me on their side, which led to arguments every time.

"I don't think I need to have an opinion," I said in exasperation. "I'm your prisoner."

"Oh, don't give me that," Wild Karl said. "You're also the first prisoner ever in the history of Finnish highway robbery. This is the greatest innovation since Flingers. You," he said grandly, "are a trailblazer."

Whenever he talked about robbing – and at other times as well – Wild Karl liked to use big words, which we kids didn't always understand. During these conversations, I noticed that something had changed. I stopped pretending to agree with them. I was no longer afraid of what might happen to me. I started to wonder if there might even be a job for me.

"Speed up. Catch them!" Charlie yelled.

We were gaining on a newish Vauxhall Crossland in front, not because we had a more powerful engine but because Hilda was not afraid to drive at top speed on a gravel road. The van weaved and juddered. It felt as if we were on board a plane.

"Less than two per cent of targets try to outrun us," Hellie said calmly as she tattooed a Barbie doll's leg with a needle and ink. As the others swayed in their seats, she didn't even bother to hang on. "And half of those give up as soon as they see how a little speed just gets us going."

"Yep, this one's giving it some welly," Hilda said and rolled down her window. "But we're not going to finish in second place."

Wild Karl let out an enormous battle cry, making my toes go numb. "Floor it!" he bellowed.

"With the ones who try to get away, we usually teach them an extra little lesson," Hellie said. "We take something they *really* don't want to part with."

"Like what?" I asked, trying not to notice how extremely close we were to the ditch. Hilda cut the corners so tightly, it sometimes felt as if the nearside tyres left the road.

"C'mon, give up!" Golden Pete roared. "They can't keep

running forever in that Vauxhall."

"Who was the last one," Charlie wondered. "That old guy on a fishing trip?"

"Yeah," Hellie replied. "Earlier this month, we took this guy's fishing lures. He was going, 'Boo-hoo, boo-hoo.' It was all junk. Amazing the way people get so attached to stuff."

Hellie chucked some random things into my lap from a drawer underneath the seat. A diary. A company accounts ledger. A leather cowboy hat. A bunch of figurines you could fix to a car's dashboard. Primrose's sunglasses. Mum's lemon-scented hand cream. I was surprised to see my Hello Kitty rucksack. It contained my purse, house keys, a sticking-plaster Mum had added and two spare pens. Usually my phone was in there too, but I'd been playing with it in the car so it had got left behind. It felt odd seeing my rucksack. I now had my survival kit – all the essentials Dad made sure I had before going out. It had been stolen along with me, presumably because it was pink and might have had more Barbie dolls inside. When it turned out to be worthless to the robbers, it had got lumped in with the junk.

I silently sorted through the other things for a while. I had learned another lesson, one the Robbersons might not have meant to teach me. All of these things were stolen from somewhere, I thought. All of them used to belong to someone else. They were someone's treasured possessions, and now they're here as stolen goods. As junk.

CHAPTER 5

in which a kiosk is held up and an important matter known as alien puke is discussed

"I could eat a whole kilo of liquorice laces," Charlie mused. We were lying on the back seat with our feet touching.

It was a sunny day in the last week of June. The van was moving at breakneck speed. Hilda was dressed in Mum's bikini, casually whistling and holding a cup of coffee in one hand while steering with the other.

"Or jelly beans," Hellie sighed. The last of the pick 'n' mix had run out two days ago.

"Or even assorted-flavour ones," Golden Pete said from his seat by the door. "I could eat all them fruit flavours. Specially the red 'n' green ones, innit."

"Would you swap half a kilo of liquorice laces for half a kilo of tangy worms?" Hilda asked from the driver's seat.

This was one of their games.

"Yeah, but I'd have to be in the middle of a good book," Charlie replied. "You can't chew tangy worms. The filling's the best part."

"Book!" Hellie snorted. "Some little bandit you are."

I smiled secretly at Charlie, but Hellie noticed and immediately pounced.

"How come the boss stole us another one like him? Why didn't you steal somebody like me?"

"All right, Hellie," Hilda said. "Half a kilo of jelly beans for half a kilo of toffee lorries?"

"No way," Hellie said, leafing through Primrose's magazine. "Those lorries melt into one big clump in the summer. Don't you remember from last year? You can only get them apart with scissors."

"Hellie never wants to swap anything," Charlie said bitterly. "She always thinks she's getting cheated on every trade."

"How 'bout this," Golden Pete said with a sly grin. "Swapping a kilo of those jelly beans for 200 grams of alien puke?"

Hellie sat up. "You're having a laugh!"

"You see? She won't swap." Charlie grinned.

"Sure I'd swap," Hellie said. "Any bandit with half a brain would swap anything to get hold of alien puke!"

"What's alien puke?" I asked Charlie.

"It's this sweetie mix," Charlie said. "Little bits of

different-flavoured candy mixed together. It looks horrible but tastes amazing. They don't make it any more."

As the days passed, my mood changed. I secretly began to enjoy being on the road. We'd yell, "Beach!" when we caught sight of a good swimming spot. Then Hilda would slam on the brakes, creating a cloud of dust on the dirt road. We'd park the van by a little lake or a scenic cove and have our campsite ready within five minutes: sun loungers out along the sunny side of the van and a board game set up on the folding table. Wild Karl always said the same thing as he took off his shirt – "Ahh, now to put some butter in the pan." He'd rub sun cream all over himself, plonk down into the sturdiest chair and start to snore.

Leaving was an equally casual business. Someone would shout, "Let's hit the road!" and within five minutes we'd be ready to go, the table safely stowed away, magazines stacked underneath a seat and the inflatable crocodile rolled up. "Bye bye," we'd call out to the shore. I was elated at how quickly we could be on the go again. If the tyres didn't squeal, Hellie would shout, "Get a move on!"

I started to feel that this was what I'd been looking for in my life. To get a move on. But of course I didn't let on to the Robbersons. I wasn't with them by choice. I was their prisoner, the loot from a robbery, and so I tried to look glum. Whenever I remembered.

"All right, you two," Hilda said as Hellie and Charlie started squabbling again. "We need to do another heist, otherwise we'll have a mutiny on our hands. Karl?"

Wild Karl, who'd been snoring his thundering, bandit-chief snore, awoke with a start.

"A heist!" he said, his eyes wide with excitement.

"Yes, absolutely. A heist. How about a car? A kiosk? A cottage?" Hilda wondered.

"You reckon it's time for a good old-fashioned kiosk hold-up?" Golden Pete asked excitedly. "Robbing always gets the old juices flowing, as I like to say. All we've been doing these past few days is swimming – not that I'm complaining. But a bit of robbing does wonders for a person's mood, innit."

"You check the atlas, Hellie," Hilda said. "Kiosks are marked with a K."

Hellie was still reading her magazine. Without taking her eyes off it, she rolled over on to her back and stuck her hand into a compartment next to the window. She seemed to know without looking which storage pocket her fingers were in and where everything was.

The 'atlas' Hilda mentioned was a large notebook with

a black cover that had sections of a map pasted inside it. Reluctantly Hellie shifted her gaze from her magazine and licked her finger, which was not particularly clean. She began paging through the notebook.

"Look in the K section," Hilda said. She expertly overtook a car on the narrow road. Karl beeped the horn with glee. The posh family car beeped back, and the father at the wheel shook his fist.

"Let's rob them!" Charlie piped up. "Prepare the Flingers!"

"No time now," Hilda said. "We're in the middle of something."

"See, lad, we're doing a kiosk heist," Golden Pete assured him. "They've got a special glamour about 'em. A touch of the big time."

Innit, I added in my mind.

"K as in kiosk. It comes after kidnapping," Hilda explained patiently to Hellie. She cranked the steering wheel to avoid an oncoming truck. I didn't know anyone who was such a reckless driver. She wasn't afraid of lorries or sharp bends on dirt roads or anything.

Hellie turned to the right page in the notebook. She glanced up at the blue signs to see what the nearest big city was and then turned some more pages. I saw that every page had a map with a picture of a red roadside kiosk stuck to it.

"Found one," Hellie said. "Two kilometres. One of those lay-bys for lorries, no buildings nearby. And I saw you," she added, turning to face me. "You're trying to spy, prisoner!"

"There will be NO more name-calling in here. It stops right now," Wild Karl said, now fully awake. "Maisie is still plenty useful to us. Go on, say it."

"All right, no more name-calling," Hellie said with a bored expression. She picked up the magazine again. Just then, she really reminded me of Primrose. "I'm, like, so sorry," she said, rolling her eyes because she knew no one in the front seat could see. "SUPER sorry."

The van was going faster than before, if that was even possible.

"Hellie's always like that," Charlie said in a quiet voice, once he saw that she was absorbed in her magazine again. "She wants everybody to be afraid of her. She wants to be a punk singer when she grows up, or the captain of a van like this, and in both of those jobs it's really important to inspire fear."

"What type of vehicle is this?" I asked Charlie. I wanted to change the subject because I was afraid Hellie would hear us and get even angrier. "At first I thought it was a people carrier – my big-headed uncle's got one sort of like it, but this one's got seats facing each other, plus the Flingers. It's strange."

"Our dad kitted it out like this," Charlie said. "He knows all there is to know about cars."

From the expression on his face I could see he wasn't telling the whole story.

"Is this a police van?" I asked.

"No." Charlie laughed. "That'd be a good one. A police van that goes round robbing people. We could paint 'Emergency Robbery Services' on the outside."

"This is a personnel transport vehicle," Golden Pete said proudly. "Seven-seater. Best fuel efficiency you can get, even with a full load. Good acceleration. Maybe a person shouldn't brag –" he paused to spit over his shoulder out of the window – "but this is quite simply the ultimate bandit van."

Hilda drove along a forest track and turned into a small lay-by. There was pine forest all around. The kiosk, with its front window propped open, stood on its own. Signs reading STRAWBERRIES and SWEETS swung in the breeze as a teenage boy struggled to unhook them.

"All right, fella?" Golden Pete said as he got out of the van. "Need some help there?" He had adopted a casual stance. Golden Pete admired refined bandits who could make everyone obey them.

"If you could give me a hand taking these down," the boy said. "They're really heavy."

I watched through the open rear door of the van as

they took the signs down. Maybe they were sold out of strawberries.

Hellie slid out after Golden Pete to stretch her legs. Refined robbery took too much time when people were gasping for sweets. Wild Karl calmly removed his seat belt and headed over to check that everything was going according to plan.

"Well then," the boy said once he was back inside the kiosk. "How can I help you? If it's coffee you're after, you'll have to wait a bit while I brew a new pot."

"We're interested in your sweets," Wild Karl said.

"And we're not in the habit of paying," Golden Pete said, adding a touch of menace to his voice. "I'm sure you understand."

They all leaned into the kiosk looking threatening, especially Hellie, who picked her teeth with a knife. I had to admit she looked really impressive.

"Suits me," the boy said.

"Me too," Wild Karl said, pleased. "I'm glad we could reach that conclusion."

"You see, this kiosk is only open for another two hours. Then that shutter is coming down, never to open again," the boy said. "There's no real passing traffic here, just holidaymakers. Everybody else takes the motorway."

"Give us the sweets!" Hellie growled.

"Come in and see what you want," the boy said, opening the side door. "They haven't sold and most of them are past their sell-by date so I shouldn't really sell them anyway. You'll be helping me clear the place out. Take whatever you like."

He leaned against a metal bin while Golden Pete, Wild Karl and Hellie carried jumbo-sized containers of liquorice, chocolate bars and jelly beans to the van.

"Ask if he's got any mustard," Hilda called out from the driver's seat. The engine was still running, even though the boy didn't look like he was going to call the police. "We've only got two tubes left."

The boy shook his head. "There was a burger van here last year but it's gone now. They towed it away at the end of last summer. I miss having someone to talk to."

The floor of the bandit van was full of boxes, most of them half empty.

"Let's go," Hellie said, drawing a line across her throat. "Seriously, people. This is SOOO lazy. Our reputation is going to suffer."

"This lad isn't going to phone anyone," Wild Karl said. "He's on our side."

"No, I won't ring the police," the teenager said, shaking his head. Then, after everyone had climbed into the van, he called out, "Hey, do you want these lollies as well? There are fifteen different flavours."

Hellie signalled to Charlie to get out and fetch the tub of lollipops.

"Can we give you a lift anywhere?" Wild Karl asked.

"No thanks," the boy replied. "I'm supposed to stay open for another couple of hours yet. My bike's over there."

"Have a nice day then," Wild Karl shouted as Hilda revved the engine. Caught up in the swell of warm feelings, I waved too.

"What a lame heist," Hellie said as the van sped off, as if there really was someone on our tail. "Some poxy chocolate bars and boxes of stuff past its sell-by date."

When she tipped the sweets out of the boxes, we noticed what a small pile they made on the floor of the van.

"But we did it all refined, like city slickers," Golden Pete said. "Textbook-style for the new kid here."

"No, it was totally cringey," Hellie said, glancing at me. "It wasn't even a real robbery. It's not actually that easy."

"This is only going to last us a couple of days," Charlie said.

I knew how many sweets the Robbersons could consume. Charlie was not exaggerating.

I had definitely eaten too much chocolate. Maybe the chocolate from the kiosk was off – my tummy was now churning. I dozed briefly and woke up in my own room. I was underneath my duvet and saw the lamp decorated with pictures of roses and carnations. It felt as if I'd slept all night. At any rate, I was at home. The whole adventure had just been a dream.

"Maisie, did you steal my hairspray?" Primrose demanded, bursting into the room. "The glitter one. I'm going to a party and I need it RIGHT NOW."

She rushed over to my bed and started shaking me by the shoulders. Now I remembered what it was like at home. Exactly like this.

"I … don't … like … hair … spray," I blurted as my head bounced back and forth. "Stop it!"

"Thief! Give it back!"

At that moment, I noticed that the voice didn't belong to Primrose but to a far fiercer being: Hellie.

I opened my eyes and saw that the bandit van had come to a stop. We had parked up but no one had bothered to wake me. The side door was open and I could hear Charlie and Hellie tussling outside. I stood up and blinked a few times. I felt happy to wake up here, to this commotion, in the front garden of an unfamiliar summer cottage. To this exciting day, which was now my life.

"Go and get your own knife," Hellie said and tackled Charlie. "Bandits don't steal from other bandits!"

"Oh yes they do," Golden Pete chuckled as he fetched a hammer from the tool bag inside the van.

"Mornin'," he said to me. "You must've had a nightmare. You were flailing about, innit. There's hot chocolate indoors if you want some."

"You've GOT your own knife," Hellie said when she saw how let down Charlie was after losing the fight.

"It's only a potato peeler," Charlie said in a small voice. "Mum said it's for vegetables. You can't use it to rob cars."

"Let's see if there's one in the kitchen," Hellie said. Charlie's face brightened and they ran off towards the log cabin.

"Hold it right there," Golden Pete said. "This place is different. Nobody's stealin' nothing from here. Not even a spoon."

I climbed out of the van. My legs were still a bit wobbly.

"Be quick," Wild Karl said as he approached Golden Pete. He had on a bathrobe I hadn't seen before. "The water's cold enough to freeze your knackers. Got to nail it on the first try, in one go."

"Yep, but it's tough when it wobbles," Golden Pete said. "It could eat a fella."

How odd. I went to look for Hilda, to see if she could explain.

"The boys are building a pontoon jetty," Hilda said before I had a chance to ask. She handed me a mug of hot chocolate. It was the perfect temperature – steaming, but not hot enough to burn your tongue. "There's that, then we need to fix the door on the outside loo and we can be off."

She drummed her fingers on a list that lay on the oilcloth-covered tabletop. The list was written in an old person's fine handwriting and continued on to the other side of the paper. When Hilda noticed me watching her, she picked up the list and put it in the pocket of her shorts.

"We'll be ready to leave soon."

"So this isn't a cottage robbery?" I asked. "I've heard about those."

"No-o-o." Hilda laughed. "Well, yes, they happen. But this is more of a fix-it job."

"A squirrel built its nest in the roof space," Hellie said as she came in for her hot chocolate. "We cleared it out and nailed the loose board back in place. There's debris and insulation scattered about. I don't know if that will affect the heating later on."

"Thank you, sweetie," Hilda said, ruffling Hellie's hair as she went past. Hellie wriggled away, but I could see from her expression how pleased she was.

"It's done," Wild Karl said as he came in, accompanied by Golden Pete. "I swear that lake gets colder every year, what with its granite bottom."

"The old dear must freeze if she goes swimming here with no sauna," Hellie said.

"I always hope we don't have to come here when it's cold," Charlie said. "This place is the coldest of them all in winter. When we're here in the snow, every time I have to brush my teeth it feels like my teeth are going to fall out. Like chunks of ice."

"All right, here's some hot chocolate for Charlie, then I'll wash up and we can head out," Hilda interrupted briskly.

I stood there in the middle of this granny's kitchen, looking like a human question mark, but none of them wanted to tell me what was going on.

The hot chocolate was finished off and soon we had packed everything into the van and were back on the road. To the steady hum of the van, I made notes in my diary.

THE BANDITS' FIX-IT JOBS
Noted down by Maisie

1. The bandit family go to a cottage where there is a list of tasks for them to do.
2. So somebody knows the Robbersons will be going there. They must be friends (NB: the letter).
3. The tasks involve getting the cottage ready for summer after the winter.
4. They have done tasks in previous years as well. (Karl Robberson's remark about the lake getting colder every year is proof of this.)
5. The person who lives in the cottage is elderly and female.
6. Has the old lady met the Robbersons, or do they just work for her?
7. Does the old lady know what the Robbersons really do? Is she sheltering highway robbers?

8. Hilda Robberson called these 'fix-it jobs'. Why on earth would a family that lives by stealing do this sort of work?

9. Charlie said this place was the coldest of all. Are there other cottages they fix up, and if so, why?

10. Why did Charlie say they sometimes visit the cottage when it's cold? Very weird. To think about later or find out: where do the Robbersons usually spend their winters?

I sucked on the end of my pencil. I couldn't get any further with the information available.

"What are you writing?" Hellie asked. She had been edging closer to me without my noticing. She came within a whisker of seeing what I'd been writing before I snapped the diary shut.

"Just making plans," I said.

"She's making plans," Wild Karl said approvingly and then turned to lecture the others. "See, she's an-a-lyzing. Drawing up schemes. Refining our operations. Who knows, there might be a new signature crime brewing in that little noggin," he said, tapping his nose. "I'm starting to get a sense of this girl. She's got mischief in mind."

Then he broke into a grin so wide, it felt as if the sun was shining inside the van.

CHAPTER 6
in which Maisie becomes a proper bandit

"Hey, there's something about you in here," Wild Karl said, waving a stolen newspaper at me. The kiosk heist was two days ago and both Hellie and Hilda seemed unimpressed with the standard of robbing there.

The folding chairs were out again for dinner. Hilda was lighting the campfire while Charlie opened packets of sausages and put out some discs of crispbread. *How nice*, I thought, *that the crispbread isn't broken up into tiny bits, so everyone can eat a huge slab piled high with food.* Hellie walked past and snatched the newspaper from Wild Karl's hand. She began reading aloud in a newsreader's voice: "*Ten-year-old Maisie still missing: The fate of Maisie Meadow Vainisto, who vanished one week ago, remains unknown. Her mother misses her terribly. Members of the public with information on her whereabouts are asked to ring…"*

"Poor dear," Hellie sneered. "Does little Maisie Meadow miss her mummy too? You must do, since it's printed in an actual newspaper."

"Missing," I snorted. "Missing! That sounds as if I'd gone out to play in the garden and was too stupid to find my way back home." I picked up a penknife and Hellie's paper target from the table and went to practise my knife-throwing. I was so furious that the first throw travelled a really long way. Sadly it didn't land anywhere near the target or even the tree.

"It woulda been nice if they'd come right out and said the girl got stolen. That's what happened at the end of the day. Stolen in broad daylight," Golden Pete mused. "Then at the Summer Shindig we could rock up and be all cool, like, 'Oh yeah, that was us in the paper. That's just how we roll, stealin' cars, robbin' kiosks, kidnappin'. That's what it's like when you're famous.'"

"Even the Farnabys' mouths would be hanging open," Wild Karl said. He picked up his copy of *National Geographic*, which he was struggling through with the help of a dictionary. "They're always going on about their famous ancestors' legacy. Any other bandit families are lucky to get a word in edgeways."

"It's high time somebody shut that young Farnaby's

mouth," Hilda said. "Ideally for good."

"Well, at least the knife's going in the right general direction now," Hellie's voice came from behind me. She had been standing there, watching me. It always amazed me how quiet her footsteps were.

"They don't even want me back," I fumed. "They're embarrassed I got stolen. That's why they didn't mention it in the paper."

Just then, the knife flew in exactly the right direction. I could tell as soon as it left my hand. It sailed towards the tree and sank into the bottom corner of the target. It was still some way off the black bullseye, but at least it was on the paper.

"There's hope for you yet," Hellie said.

That was the most positive thing she'd ever said to me. Then she pulled the knife out of the tree and started throwing it at the target over her shoulder without looking, as if to show me what a depressingly long way I still had to go.

That evening we played Yahtzee, which we did every night. It's a game you play with five dice. You roll the dice to get different combinations, like rolling as many threes as possible, or trying to make the highest total. We played just before bed to decide who got to sleep where. The winner got the big bed in the bandit van and could choose who would share it with them. The losers had to go in the tent. Now that Golden Pete was no longer keeping watch over me at night, he had gone back to sleeping in his hammock. He would string the hammock up between two trees or on hooks inside the van if it was raining. I had slept with Charlie and Hellie in the tent every night except the first, when Pete had guarded me.

"Big house!" Wild Karl shouted in excitement, doing the pot-stirring dance he always did when he was happy. "Big house, big house, who's got a big house? Me, that's who!"

He'd shout the same thing and dance his silly dance every night. I was just learning the rules, checking the dog-eared rulebook to see what I should try for next. The rulebook said a full house (which I guess Wild Karl meant when he said 'big house') was three dice showing one number plus two dice of another number.

"Sorry, that's not a full house," I said.

"Oh yes it is," Golden Pete said quickly with a strange, wide-eyed expression.

"Yes indeed," Hilda echoed. "It is, just look." She cleared her throat meaningfully.

"No, it isn't," I said, surprised. "That's a three. It would have to be a two."

"It's a full house," Hellie said, about to gather the dice in the cup for her turn. "Some people are just lucky."

"But—" I said, pointing to the page about a full house.

Charlie took the rulebook from my hands and gave me the same look as Golden Pete. Quick as a flash, Wild Karl stopped Hellie picking up the dice and checked what he had rolled.

"Maisie's right. It's not a big house. That's a three." He looked disappointed, before adding, "You all tricked me into thinking I got it. Everybody but Maisie."

"It looked like a two in this light, Boss," Charlie reassured him.

"The main thing is that we finish the game," Hilda said to calm things down. "It's getting chilly and we need to know where everybody's going to sleep tonight. Your turn to roll the dice, Hellie."

I imagined what it would feel like to snuggle up with a soft pillow. The best thing about sleeping in the van was that you got proper sheets and a blanket. In the tent you needed a sleeping bag because it was so cold.

"You all thought I couldn't handle losing!" Wild Karl shouted. He clawed at one of his braids, which came undone. "What kind of scam are you running here? And with your own boss!"

Hellie rolled and scored herself a zero for that turn. I thought her sigh of disappointment seemed over the top. What was going on?

"It's Maisie's go," she said in Wild Karl's direction.

"She needs to get Yahtzee to win – it's not easy to get five of a kind. Looks like you're going to win again, Boss. I guess we kids need to improve our wrist action. It's all in the wrist, right?"

"It is all in the wrist. What did I say, Pete?" Wild Karl said, relieved.

Golden Pete quickly agreed.

I rolled the dice and got three fives. On my two additional throws, I got two more fives. Yahtzee, I noted on my scorecard. Fifty points. I had achieved every combination on my scorecard, and my final score was higher than Wild Karl's.

"Finished. Looks like I win," I said with a smile.

"I see," Wild Karl replied. He blinked. "So Maisie wins."

Everyone stared at me. It was deathly silent.

"Congratulations," Hilda said as she pulled her cardigan round her more tightly. The evening had grown cool. "Do you mind sleeping in our old bedding? We have some more in that chest, but it would be nice to save them for the Summer Shindig."

"No, that's fine," I said. "It'll be nice just to have proper sheets."

Charlie gave me a kick in the shin.

"Who are you going to be sharing with?" Hilda asked gently. She seemed to be nodding in the direction of Wild Karl, who was gathering up the little dice in his huge hand to put them away.

"You win some, you lose some," Wild Karl muttered as he closed the box.

"I thought maybe Charlie," I said.

Charlie gave me another kick.

"And Hellie too, I guess," I added quickly. "I think we'll all fit. The bed's pretty wide."

Hellie poked me in the back. "Actually, I'm not planning on going to sleep tonight," she said. "I've always thought I ought to see the sunrise. Yeah. I want to think about our next heists and watch the sun come up. I'll just take that quilt and sit in a chair."

They all seemed to be edging away from me.

"Good idea, Hellie," Golden Pete said. "I'll go outside too. My hammock and me have spent many great nights together. I bet I wouldn't sleep a wink stretched out straight."

He took a grey cardboard box and his rolled-up hammock from the luggage rack and went outside.

"You won't get him inside," Charlie said. "He works on secret projects at night when nobody else is up to see what he's doing."

"What's he making?" I asked, intrigued.

Charlie shook his head. "It has to stay a secret until the Summer Shindig. And don't peek inside the box, unless you want to suffer a painful death. Golden Pete is easy-going about everything except that."

"Well, then," Hilda said briskly, dusting off her hands. "Time for bed. Charlie and Maisie in the van, and let's get a quilt for Hellie. Karl, you grab that sleeping bag and we'll head over to the tent." She started to lead her husband towards the tent. It was pitched next to the birch tree where Hellie's knife was still sticking out of the trunk.

As we were crawling under the covers in the van, Charlie hissed, "You're supposed to let him win!"

"How come?" I whispered back. Charlie didn't answer, just busied himself making a nest of pillows.

The van was super cosy at night. A slatted base had been pulled out from under one of the seats. When placed between the two long seats, it created a space the size of a double bed. Soft music was playing on the radio. You could close the curtains. The fading evening sunlight cast shadows of the Barbie dolls with nooses round their necks on the curtains.

We'd been lying in bed for a while, staring at the ceiling of the van, when Charlie said, "You know, sometimes I think I'd give anything to be you."

"Really?" I asked in astonishment. "Why's that?"

"At some point you'll get to go back home. To your own life," he explained.

"That's nothing to look forward to," I told him. I remembered what it was like to argue with Primrose every day and every evening while Dad sat at his laptop and

Mum cooked dinner, talking on her phone. They always told us not to bother them because they were busy. As if we didn't matter.

"Do you have your own room?" Charlie asked.

"Yeah," I said. I thought about my room, which was always perfectly neat and tidy. Even my dolls were arranged in order of height, although I never really played with them any more. On my desk I had one pot filled with regular pencils and another with coloured pencils, all sharpened to a fine point. Then I thought about Primrose, who was always nicking stuff from my room – things she could never find in her pigsty under the piles of lip gloss, jeans and silly quizzes torn from magazines. It made me miss home a bit, and I thought it might be nice to be back in my own room. But only for a little while.

"Sounds wicked." Charlie sighed. "If I had my own room, I'd have a sign on the door telling everyone to keep out."

He closed his eyes. It looked like he was imagining the sign – with a skull and crossbones and the words: *This is Spine-Chilling Charlie's territory. Enter at your own risk.* I wondered what Charlie would have in his room. Pirate ships? A bedside table shaped like a treasure chest? Pictures of legendary bandits?

With his eyes still closed, he said, "I reckon we'll give you back when summer's over. You'll have to go back to school in the autumn, and during the winter it gets cramped with all of us in the van at night."

"Yeah," I said.

It felt odd talking about my normal life when I wasn't sure I'd ever be able to go back to it, or even want to. Remembering certain things reminded me that now I was on a genuine adventure.

"I'd like to go to school too," Charlie said, his eyes open. "Hellie always teases me when I try to read something. I have lots of books, but they've all got holes in from Hellie's knife."

We were silent for a long time. I wiggled my toes under the blanket. The van felt like a safe place, where I could say anything.

Finally I worked up the courage to ask again, "How come I was supposed to let Karl win?" I sensed it was the right moment to get some answers.

"Dad gets a bad back if he sleeps in the tent," Charlie said, "and then the rest of us suffer the next day."

Charlie sprang up from under the covers and peered out of the window towards the tent, making sure his parents weren't listening in on our conversation. "Hellie's asleep in her chair." He giggled. "So much for her sunrise."

"But why do you still play a game to decide where you sleep every night?" I asked, confused. "If Wild Karl always has to win, I mean?"

Charlie crawled back under the covers next to me and

sighed happily as he settled into a comfy pillow. "What? Not play? Dad would never agree to that. It would be like giving up," he said. He looked at my astonished expression, then started to laugh. "You see, Dad's afraid he'd look like a wimp if he automatically got to sleep in his favourite spot every night. I guess we bandits are a bit odd."

We both giggled.

"Just imagine: assigned places for everybody to sleep," he said. "What's exciting or bandit-like about that?"

Charlie soon fell asleep, curled up tight. He started to snore gently. I found myself thinking about the Robberson family and then, suddenly, about my own family. Thoughts raced around my head until I got up and wrote them down.

BACKGROUND TO THE PERFECT CRIME
Noted down by Maisie

1. Nobody's tried to get me back, which is embarrassing and makes me furious.
2. Mum and Dad should be made to pay a ransom - that's the only way they'll understand I was really taken.
3. The ransom should be in the form of sweets or food - something that's useful for the Robbersons.
4. The amount of ransom should be suitably big.
5. The method of payment mustn't put the Robbersons in danger.

After writing down my thoughts, I had the best night's sleep, better than I'd ever had at home. The van seemed to protect us from Wild Karl's snoring. I dreamed vivid dreams in which I waved an old-fashioned pistol around and robbed kiosks. I sailed on a pirate ship and climbed up to the top of the mast.

After three adventurous dreams, I woke up and realized I'd found the solution to my problem. Charlie was still fast asleep, mumbling into his pillow. I had come up with a plan. A plan that would give my family what they deserved for not trying hard enough to find me.

Breakfast the next morning was quiet.

"I can't have any meatballs," Wild Karl moaned. He did look a bit pale. "I'd need to open my mouth wide, but my back won't let me. How can I start my morning with no meatballs?"

"Your back doesn't stop you eating," Hilda said cheerfully as she cracked some more eggs into the sizzling pan.

"Yes it does," Wild Karl grumbled, glaring at us. Then he turned to Hilda. "And you got to sleep on the soft side, where there was all grass and wildflowers. I had to lie on the tree roots." His tone sounded pitiful and he grimaced every time he shifted in his chair.

"We swapped places, remember?" Hilda said. "You wanted

to sleep on that side." She almost sang the last sentence.

Wild Karl hardly ate anything. He just sat and sulked about his empty belly. Then he growled, "Tell me, whose idea was it to pitch the tent right there?"

"Yours," Charlie answered quietly, staring at his slice of bread.

"Hey," I said, once the bandit van was loaded and we were on our way to our next destination, "what do you think about pulling an even bigger heist than the kiosk robbery?"

"Oh, so YOU'RE going to start thinking up heists for us now, are you?" Hellie sneered, although she looked quite interested. She pretended to be busy cutting up a magazine, but she made sure she didn't miss a word of our conversation.

"What sort of heist?" Hilda asked. "Where should we go? We're starting to run low on supplies. We should stock up on sandwich fillings and other things in the next few days."

"OK, everybody," I said, then began to tell them about my suggested target.

By the time I was halfway through, Wild Karl had forgotten all about his bad back and began to chuckle.

CHAPTER 7
in which Maisie commits her signature crime

"Hello, Jon Vainisto speaking," came the voice on the phone.

"Hi, Dad, it's me," I said. I tried to sound scared, as if I really were being held at gunpoint. In reality, I was calling from a pay phone using some money I'd found in my Hello Kitty survival rucksack. Dad was insistent that I always had a ten-euro note with me, along with my home address and phone number written down. I also had to keep my ID card with me. "That's my girl," he'd always say. I think he was afraid I might get lost. I don't think he ever considered the possibility I could get stolen on the way to Grandma's house. That sort of thing just didn't occur in Jon Vainisto's world.

I had to make it through the phone call on my own. None of the Robbersons were listening in, as they were worried about being seen in public. Instead, they waited in the bandit van and promised to cross their fingers for me.

"If you have any information regarding our daughter, call the hotline listed in the newspaper. That number is manned around the clock. That's the only way to get the reward. This is the Vainisto family's landline number," Dad said. His voice sounded tired and robotic.

"I know, Dad. This is Maisie, your daughter who was kidnapped. Remember?" I said in an equally level tone. Then I added, "Here's a summary of the whole embarrassing story. We were on our way to visit Grandma when you let me get kidnapped. I was carried away from the car, and you guys did nothing to stop it. If this conversation isn't going anywhere, I'm going to hang up. A kidnapped person has things to do, you know."

"Maisie!" Dad gasped. "Anna! Hurry, it's Maisie!"

I heard a click as Mum picked up the extension.

"Now listen carefully," I told them. "The bandits who stole me need to hang on to me a little longer."

"Oh my word," Mum sobbed. "Our little girl is doing forced labour."

"They're treating me fine and I'm getting enough to eat," I said. "But the newspaper articles need to stop. You can say you'd forgotten I was at Grandma's in Kajaani. I mean, you're always losing track of where I am. This wouldn't be the first time."

"But that would be a lie," Dad said.

"But so is saying that I'm lost when I was actually stolen," I said firmly. It felt good to tell them that. "If those articles don't stop, the people who kidnapped me won't be responsible for the consequences. In their line of work they mustn't attract attention."

"I promise," Mum said, sounding tearful. "No more newspaper articles. We just need to keep Primrose quiet."

"Bribe her," I commanded. "And another thing. It's not exactly cheap to keep me fed. They won't necessarily go on treating me so well. You need to pay for my upkeep."

"Oh, here we go," Dad said, irritated. "Here comes the demand for money."

"Don't be so silly," I told him. "No money will change hands. The police would be able to trace it."

"Oh?" Dad said. He sounded as if he was ready to give in and do what I asked.

Brilliant, I thought gleefully. "Here are your instructions," I said.

"I've got a pen," Mum said. She was always quicker than him. "Go ahead."

"Go to that cinema chain where you've got a membership account," I said.

"What?" Dad said.

"Just listen," I said. "Open a new account in my name and tell them that because I'm underage, the bills for my account will go to you. You need to do this within the hour."

"Cinema?" Mum said, confused. "Are your kidnappers going to watch movies?"

"Or maybe I will," I said. "We get breaks during our forced labour."

I could hear the sound of a pen on paper as Mum scribbled down the instructions.

"You mustn't tell the police about this, or Primrose, or anyone else," I said. "Otherwise something might happen to me. You guys go there all the time anyway. You need to pay the bill every week – no matter how much it is."

"I don't know if this is going to work," Dad said.

"It will work," I told him. "You've got a lot of influence, Dad, and you can use your connections." Then I turned away and pretended to sound afraid. "Hey! Stop pointing that gun at me. I've done everything you asked me to." I spoke into the receiver again and said, "Dad, Mum, you've got to do as I said. My life is in danger!"

"Oh my God," Mum said, her voice filled with terror.

"And one more thing," I said. "The bills might show what towns we've visited, but you mustn't try to find me. So long as you don't come looking for me, you'll get me back in one piece. Probably at the end of summer."

"Will you cope, darling?" Mum asked.

"I'll have to," I said bravely, just as I started to get a funny feeling in my tummy.

"All sorted," I said back inside the bandit van. Wild Karl was wiping his forehead with a hanky the size of half a bed sheet. "Were you scared?" I asked.

He looked pale all over, even the tip of his nose. "Nah, my back's just giving me a bit of trouble," he fibbed. He nodded to Hilda to start up the van.

"Were *you* scared?" Hellie asked me as we zoomed off towards the nearest town. I shook my head.

Hilda seemed nervous as we drove round the town centre. At each traffic light, she revved the engine and tugged at the straps on her top.

"Sunglasses," she said in a low voice. "Karl, can you fetch me the mirrored sunglasses from the glove compartment? And Hellie, give your father the baseball cap that's on that hook. The rest of you, stay well back from the windows. For some reason, this van is attracting a lot of attention."

Hilda was exaggerating. Plenty of people were out and about on that summer's day, going about their business. Old people had shopping bags filled with spring onions and new potatoes from the outdoor market. Some kids were queuing by an ice-cream van. Families cycled towards the lake with their swimming things. Nobody was really interested in our black van, even with the Barbie dolls hanging by their necks in the windows.

In the distance I could see the familiar logo of the cinema chain.

"There it is." I pointed. "By the car park for that shopping centre."

"Too many folks around for my liking," Golden Pete said. "No good for robbing people."

"We're not going to hit a car," I declared. "This is a brand-new method."

Hilda parked the van as close to the cinema entrance as she could get. "Should I keep the engine running?" she asked. "Will we need to make a quick getaway?"

"Actually, no," I said.

I saw her face droop. Then I added, "Maybe switch off the engine, but keep the key in the ignition. And make sure nobody takes too much notice."

The usual glint returned to Hilda's eyes.

"The rest of you, come with me," I said.

"What, even me?" Charlie asked in astonishment. "Go in there?"

"Well, I'm not going to be able to carry all the loot out on my own," I said.

The deserted cinema foyer livened up when our odd bunch walked through the doors. The little bell above the door nearly frightened the life out of Golden Pete. He froze in the entry between the sets of inner and outer doors until I calmed him down and got him into the foyer. This cinema looked like any other, with a ticket counter and posters for the latest films. In addition to a counter where you could buy popcorn and drinks, the shop had a pick 'n' mix section filled with sweets. The sweets were on two rows of low shelves. Each kind was in a separate clear plastic cube with a lid. You could scoop the sweets into paper bags, which were piled at the end of the aisle.

The Robbersons needed some time to take in just how many sweets there were.

"Banana rafts," Wild Karl said as his jaw dropped.

"Liquorice ropes," sighed Charlie.

"Salty liquorice bugs," Hellie said. Even Hellie sounded vaguely impressed. I saw that as an achievement.

"I reckon I've died and gone to heaven," Golden Pete said. "This must be candy paradise."

"I'll handle this," I told them. I skipped up to the popcorn till, hoping I looked like an ordinary kid. Summery. I knew the Robbersons were all watching me.

"Hello," I said. "I'd like to check the status of an account, please. My name is Maisie Meadow Vainisto and my dad has opened an account for me."

"Sorry, what?" the guy at the till said. He was listening to music on his headphones. He pushed them back on his head to hear what I was saying.

I repeated my request, then added, "My dad was incredibly nice to do this for me," in a single breath, trying to appear more innocent and cuter than I really am. I felt myself getting super nervous. I wanted to fidget with all the things on the counter to calm myself down. I continued, "I'm spending the summer up here and he's busy down in Helsinki, so this means I can buy stuff and Daddy will pay. Isn't that handy? Here's my ID. Can you check that the account is open?"

"We don't have that kind of account," the guy grunted.

I'm not going to pull this off, I thought and gulped. A cold feeling filled my tummy. It wasn't going to work. Then I felt angry. *Primrose would never wimp out*, I thought. I was being a wimp. Primrose always got what she wanted. So I put on my very best Primrose act.

"Pleeeeathe," I said with a Primrose-style lisp. "I'm, like, totally sure it's in the system."

I smiled and leaned against the counter. Primrose would have flicked her hair, but I couldn't go that far. Anyway, it worked. Looking bored, the assistant tapped my ID number into the till. Then his expression changed and he said, "It's here. Well, what do you know?!"

"Daddy works for the government," I said with a grin, celebrating as Maisie rather than as Primrose. Then I turned to the others and told them, "Go for it!"

Hilda couldn't believe her eyes when we started bringing

out paper bags stuffed to the brim with sweets. There was one whole bag with just banana rafts and toffee lorries – the ultimate combination. A bag of raspberry boats for Hilda. Two bags of liquorice rope and another filled with regular liquorice. There were only enough salty liquorice bugs for half a bag, but the assistant brought out more from the stock room so we filled up that bag as well.

I stood close to the till so the Robbersons couldn't see what was going on there. I gestured wildly so they might think I was being threatening, but I was actually just pointing at the posters behind the till and speaking nicely to the assistant.

"These as well. And these. And these," I said.

The poor guy. I kept hoisting bags of sweets on to the scale by the basketful. We usually used that basket to carry our swimming things, but it worked just as well for bags of sweets. The assistant had to weigh one basketful of sweets after another. He kept punching numbers into the till. Then I handed the basket to whoever's turn it was to carry it out to the van. Everyone else kept scooping sweets into more bags. Once the basket had been unloaded in the van, it got filled up again. Nobody paid much attention to me – the Robbersons were focused on the sweets. Golden Pete sobbed with delight every time he came across varieties he'd only tasted once before. Old-fashioned creamy fudge! Chocolate-filled liquorice sticks!

Melting mushrooms!

We must have had around a hundred bags. We'd used up all the paper bags in the aisle, so for foamy sweets we switched to plastic bags. It actually might have been more like 150 bags. Sometimes the assistant got confused about which ones he'd already weighed. In the end, he just waved his hands and said, "Just take what you want, it doesn't matter." The total on the till appeared to be a three-digit number. I hoped it was at least 200 euros or even more. I was worth that much.

And this was only the beginning.

"So then this little lady marches up to the till and says, 'Put yer hands up, this is a robbery,'" Golden Pete said when the van was well out of town. "She slammed the bags on the counter and hissed some fearsome threats to the fella. Just like the big time. Real calm, the way it should be done. If anybody had been stood next to her they wouldn't have heard a thing. A textbook robbery!"

"It wasn't quite like that," I smiled. Golden Pete made me sound like a hardened criminal who went round robbing sweetie shops.

"Well, how did you do it?" Hellie asked, popping a sour rat and several salty liquorice bugs into her mouth at the same time. I had already copied that combination of hers, so I knew what an amazing taste sensation it was. "What did you actually say to the guy?" she pressed.

"It's a secret," I said. "What I can tell you is that I also laid the groundwork for a follow-up. Once we've eaten this lot, we can top up in any large town."

"Our Maisie has got herself a signature crime," Wild Karl said with emotion in his voice. "Ten years old and she's lent her name to a whole new type of crime. A remarkable achievement. Look what good teachers we are, Hilda!"

Hellie looked envious. Charlie gave her a little kick and said, "This one's trying to steal ideas. She wants to copy Maisie instead of coming up with her own."

"Actually, I already have a signature crime. I robbed a convertible by dropping down from a tree right in front of it," Hellie said.

"Yes, you did," Hilda responded in a frosty voice. "And you're never going to do it again. It was lucky they stopped and didn't run you over."

"A signature crime," Wild Karl said. He started to get carried away recalling his first car heists with Golden Pete. Suddenly he said, "Maisie, you deserve a party. How about some cake?"

"Isn't a whole van filled with sweets enough of a party?" Hellie said, sulking. Then we all burst out laughing.

CHAPTER 8

in which Operation Captain's Coat is launched

After my big heist, the Robbersons started to trust me a lot more than before. Golden Pete no longer sat guarding me in case I tried to escape. Hellie had given up trying to intimidate me and had started treating me almost humanely. Wild Karl didn't lecture me on freedom and life on the road the way he had done in the first couple of weeks. He finally considered me one of them.

"The Summer Shindig is two weeks away," Hilda said one evening as we sat picking over what was left of supper. The last evenings in June were bright. The summer holidays were just beginning, and there were more people on the country roads. More people to rob. "We ought to get some more supplies," she added.

"Yay, more robbing!" Charlie said. "I want to do some

too! I'm nearly the same age as Maisie, and she's got her own signature crime. There's no age limit. It doesn't say anywhere that you have to be ten years old to go robbing! And anyway, I'll be ten this autumn."

An ominous silence descended around the folding table, the way it always did when someone tried to quibble about rules.

Not noticing the storm brewing, Charlie continued, "Besides, I'm lighter than Dad. I bet I can leap twice as far as him off the Flinger."

"What are you trying to say?" Wild Karl said in a genuinely menacing tone. "And what are you on about, Hilda? What supplies? We've got everything we need."

"Well, to be perfectly honest," she said, trying not to laugh as she kept her eyes on the road, "before we meet up with the other bandit clan bosses, you have got to get a new jacket."

"Oh, leave it out," Wild Karl said as he tugged his cardigan down over his belly. "This one's just fine. Look at those magazines we stole! Crop tops are all the rage these days."

According to Wild Karl, life without a captain's coat just wasn't worth living. In his view, it was the most important bit of kit for robbing cars or crawling under the van to check on the wire holding the silencer in place or going fishing on your day off. It was like a uniform to him. When he was out and about – robbing, going into sweet shops or just on the open road – he always had his cardigan on. He called it his 'captain's coat'. It was meant to make him look sleek.

The argument between Hilda and Wild Karl dragged on. It was still going when we pulled in to a campsite car park for a lunch break.

Hilda dragged Wild Karl off to the campsite's disabled toilet and let the full-length mirror inside do the talking. By the time they returned, it was clear he had admitted defeat. His cardigan just would not reach far enough – an expanse of belly poked out below.

"I told you to start swimming regularly," Hilda told him. "But did you?"

"Are you trying to say I'm … fat?" Wild Karl asked in a voice hinting at meltdown. "Are you trying to make me do some *exercise*?" The head of the Robberson family trembled with hurt, right down to the tiniest hairs on his arms. "Are you saying I'm unfit? Am I not threatening any more? Is that what you mean?" he demanded.

Hilda gulped as she tried to think of a reply. "Well, no," she began. "What I meant was… What *did* I mean?"

For the first time, I thought Hilda seemed uncertain. When she was at the wheel of the van, she always knew what to do.

"We'd better get out of here," Charlie whispered to me.

"Quick, come up with a reason!" I said.

"Y'see," Golden Pete jumped in, "what Miss Hilda *meant* to say is that you can stretch yer jacket into shape if ya soak it first, good and wet, like."

Wild Karl's face brightened. He took off his cardigan in under a second. Without it on, he looked even bigger – if that was even possible. 'Big' wasn't really the right word, though. He looked monumental. We definitely had Finland's most impressive bandit boss.

Wild Karl began pouring water on his cardigan.

"Come on then, stretch it!" he ordered.

Hilda tugged and pulled at the woollen fabric.

"Mmm, reckon it might be too late," Golden Pete fibbed. "Looks like it's not stretchin'. That's a real shame, innit. No way out now. Should've done it at the start of summer. Now the fibres are already froze in place."

"Puh-leease," Hellie said, rolling her eyes exactly the way Primrose does.

"Good job you know so much about fabrics, Pete," Hilda said with a glint in her eye. "You'll have no trouble dealing with this."

She dropped the balled-up cardigan into Golden Pete's hands. His face went pale.

"Excuse me," Hellie said, looking up from the Barbie doll she'd recently stolen, which she was customizing with black nail varnish for eye shadow. "Why don't you just get a new one?"

"I hereby declare the planning meeting for Operation Captain's Coat open," Wild Karl announced. He was holding a crispbread sandwich in one hand and chomped half of it in one bite.

"Puh-leease," Hellie repeated. "Why don't we just go and hold up a couple of cars, ransack them and get you a new jacket?"

"Yeah! I'll get to wave my knife and go, 'Give us your jacket'," Charlie said in a blood-curdling voice that made Hellie giggle. "Well, what would *you* say? 'Would you be so kind as to hand over your garment, good sir?'"

"Excuse me, sir, we require all your clothing," Hellie added, getting swept up in the fun. "Pleasure doing business with you, see you again soon, *au revoir*."

"You kids just don't get it," Wild Karl said in a hurt voice. "A captain's coat is important. On summer days, when a person's life and reputation are at stake, it's VITALLY important. It's a matter of credibility. Remember item two on the list of bandit trademarks – looks!"

He looked at me and gave me a kind of signal. It dawned on me what he meant, so I quickly leafed through my notes. Then I read aloud:

2) Looks
A bandit's credibility depends on their appearance. A politician has to look like a politician. A bandit has to look like a bandit. You can't leave any doubt in your target's mind as to whether it's a fancy-dress party or a hold-up. A sense of fear generates a desire to cooperate, which helps speed

up the robbery process. That in turn reduces the chance of getting caught.

"There you have it," Wild Karl said, then swallowed the rest of his sandwich. "A bandit chief can't just wear any old thing. A real bandit chief has to be blood-chilling. *Blood-chill-ing.*"

As he repeated it, Wild Karl made a grand, sweeping gesture.

"Another example," he continued. "Look here." He opened the copy of *National Geographic* they'd stolen some time ago. "This is what a ship's captain looks like. A man who sails the high seas. There aren't many ship's captains – they're just as rare as bandit chiefs. So it's important that their clothes make them instantly identifiable. Bandit chiefs are endangered, like the rainforests and snow leopards."

Wild Karl's presentation carried on for so long that everyone sat back in their folding chairs – even Charlie. I took notes.

"What's the most important quality a cardigan – I mean captain's coat – should have?" I asked.

"Good question! Very good question," Wild Karl said. He began pacing back and forth like a teacher, but no ideas occurred to him. He mumbled the question to himself in the hope his brain would spring into action, but it refused. His desperation made his voice shrill and loud. He flung his braids. He sounded like an opera singer warming up.

"What's the most impoooortant? Mo-mo-mo-mohhhst. What's the most impoooortant?"

Everyone racked their brains. Hilda pushed a lock of hair behind her ear. Golden Pete felt the sleeve of his own jacket and silently mouthed some words. An idea occurred to Hellie and she started to raise her hand to speak. Wild Karl saw her and turned his back to her. He wanted to be the one to answer this question.

"What qualities does it need to have?" he wondered, then turned to me with a triumphant look. "Take this down."

Hellie waved her arm wildly and clicked her fingers to get his attention, but Wild Karl came and sat down between her and me. "It needs to be black. With long sleeves. Not too warm," he listed.

"Is that it?" I blurted.

Everyone's eyes were fixed on me like a thousand sharp knives.

"I mean ... great list," I said hurriedly. "Good stuff ... especially those ... sleeves. Yep, sleeves are good. But why black?"

More scolding looks. Hilda shook her head, showing her deep disappointment.

"I'm only asking because black is usually ... warm." As soon as those words had left my mouth I felt so nervous I nearly fainted.

82

"True," Wild Karl said. "Hilda! This girl is smart!"

All of a sudden he picked me up and waved me in the air like a flag. Then he put me down with exaggerated care.

"Why you'd want to go to school I'll never know. What could they teach somebody like you there?" he wondered.

Charlie looked glum. It didn't seem like his dream of attending school would come true any time soon. Hellie, on the other hand, was overjoyed. Wild Karl's statement guaranteed her many more years of freedom on the road. Meanwhile, I wondered whether I'd ever get to go home. Would this bandit father ever give me up?

"Why black, this brilliant little wise creature asks me – the most fearsome and therefore the only true highway robber chief in the land," Wild Karl said in a sugary voice as he patted my face. His huge hand scrunched my cheeks together, making me look like a pouting fish.

"Black because, my dear friend, black is slimming. Full stop. Black is stylish. Black – and only black – creates the right impression. Blood-chill-ing," he said.

He let go of my face and adopted an extremely blood-chilling bandit-chief pose.

"That's about it," Golden Pete said, closing the meeting. "Sounds like we've got us an operation under way. Let's go out there and get us that captain's coat, innit."

That was the plan, anyway. But after three days of non-stop effort, Operation Captain's Coat still hadn't come up with the goods. Robbing cars wasn't the problem. It was fixed in the robbers' muscle memory: raise the flag, prime the Flingers, block the target's path and spring into action. The problem was in knowing who was worth targeting. There was no need to be so choosy when the objective was food. Just a couple of heists netted a whole boot load of rhubarb, new potatoes, pickled herring and fresh strawberries. Our diet was healthier than it had ever been.

Two days and six fruitful heists later, we were desperate. After each hold-up we had to floor it to a new location to avoid being spotted by the local police. The van was grey with dust from the country roads. Nobody had any appetite for this much food. All that dangling from the Flingers was for nothing.

"Maybe we should come up with a different plan. Wouldn't it be easier to rob a clothing store?" I suggested.

"You what?" Hilda replied. She seemed surprised by the idea that it was possible to get clothes other than by taking them from people.

"A bit like we did with the sweets," I said.

"Sounds complicated," Hilda said cautiously. "And Karl doesn't like anything too complicated."

"This is useless," Hellie said as she put on her swimming cap. We had found a secluded little lake to rest our overheated minds. "The weather is against us. Nobody takes a cardigan with them in this heat. At least not a black, long-sleeved one. Come on, people! Nobody's thought this through."

"Who said it would be easy?" Wild Karl said as he got out of the van wearing his home-made long-john swimming trunks. "We need some challenges."

As he dashed towards the water, he started bellowing to encourage himself. He carried on roaring all the way into the lake. Some distance away, a couple of elderly fish floated up to the surface, having died of fright.

"Really terrifying," I said to Charlie with a laugh.

I was impressed that Wild Karl was actually going for a swim as a result of Hilda's scolding. He did it each time we stopped for a break. On several occasions I noticed him looking at a photo of Captain Cousteau in his *National Geographic* magazine. He would gaze at the photo, imitate the pose and then head off to the van to change into his swimming trunks.

"You should see him when he runs the whole way from the van out to the jetty and does a bomb into the water," smiled Charlie.

I watched as Wild Karl floated on his back until he got tired and walked to shore. As he approached the edge of the water, he crouched down and continued with just his eyes above the surface, like a crocodile. He was surprisingly agile for a man of his size. Charlie let out a little squeal as

Wild Karl finally emerged from the water with a roar.

"Morale is flagging. The troops are revolting. Don't think I haven't noticed," Wild Karl said in a reptile-like voice. "But we will not give up! This is one of our basic principles! Hope!" he shouted, then tried to get the water out of one ear. His wet hair was plastered down and his braids were dripping. It made him look even sillier, if that was possible.

He continued: "It's a … ceremonial garment. For a bandit chief, you see. That other guy, what's-his-name, had to search for ages to find the Holy Kale."

"Oh yeah, what was his name?" I asked as I wrote down the term in my best handwriting: *Holy Grail.*

"Oh, who was it?" Wild Karl repeated. He was hopping on one leg with his head tilted to one side because his ear was still blocked. "That really famous bandit chief."

"King Arthur?" I ventured ever so cautiously.

"Arthur!" Wild Karl smiled. "That's him. I know the fella."

"Bet we'll meet him at the Summer Shindig," Golden Pete said with a grin that revealed his gold teeth. "Same line of work, innit."

Later, after two weeks of waiting, things started to happen – thank goodness.

"Promising-looking Salary Sam in an estate car, blue, doing eighty kilometres an hour," Hellie announced over the walkie-talkie. We were sitting in the branches of a birch tree. She was looking through binoculars with the walkie-talkie in her other hand. It crackled when a question came from the van.

"Driver alone. Right size," Hellie answered.

Another crackle.

"Birch tree, over and out," she said. She hung the binoculars round her neck, put the walkie-talkie in her back pocket and hopped down from the tree in a single skilful leap. "Yep. At last, things are happening. The old grump's finally found something he likes."

Hellie was waiting impatiently for me on the ground. We didn't have much time to get into position before the car reached us. She watched my attempt to get down, then took the walkie-talkie from her pocket and said into it, "Slight snag at the birch tree, tourist stuck, hang on."

"What on earth is a Salary Sam?" I asked, clutching the tree trunk until my knuckles turned white. Climbing up had been much easier. Eventually I made it down, but I had to keep my eyes shut the whole way.

"It's a type of person," Hellie said as we broke into a run towards the van. "They think they're completely normal, but they spend a lot of money on stuff, like cars, food, clothes. Things we like, which makes Salary Sams excellent targets for robbing."

"Were we Salary Sams?" I asked with a gasp.

"No way," Hellie said. She didn't seem out of breath at all. "Your dad is a grade-A Manager Mel. The most extreme kind. It's a wonder we stopped you at all. We must've had some time on our hands or something."

I had my work cut out keeping up with Hellie. I tried to ask more questions but was just panting. Despite all the swimming, I wasn't as fit as her.

She took pity on me. "So you were wondering about your dad. Manager Mels aren't worth robbing. Hopeless cases. They never have anything useful with them. They're obsessed with keeping their cars perfectly neat and tidy." She gave her typical laugh, which felt like a dentist's drill with no anaesthetic.

"What are you then? Do you think you're better than other people?" I demanded. Then I stopped suddenly. I knew the car would come whizzing along very soon.

Hearing her say my dad was a hopeless case was hard to take. True, he was nitpicky. And full of himself. And totally in love with that car of his...

"Who, us?" Hellie laughed. "We're highway robbers through and through."

Then we roared and ran towards the car that had whizzed past. It did an emergency stop when it met the bandit van blocking the road behind a bend. We ran, and I let out another huge roar that spooked the birds, sending them flying from the trees on both sides of the road.

CHAPTER 9
in which some unusual relatives turn up

"It's time," Hilda said as she looked at the map while the rest of us figured out where to sit in the bandit van after breakfast. That morning's breakfast had been particularly grand, because of the estate car we'd held up the previous day. In addition to a cardigan in the right size, it had contained a cool bag full of pancakes. So we had pancakes with jam for breakfast. Wild Karl had a crispbread sandwich, pancakes and bacon for his main course, followed by more pancakes for dessert. Everybody ate until they were ready to burst. Even Charlie kept going back for more, though he complained of a tummy ache. We all felt sleepy afterwards in the van.

We had started our journey north towards the Summer Shindig, and Wild Karl now had a suitable cardigan –

his captain's coat. Hilda absolutely forbade him to wear it before the event in case he got mustard on it. I had noticed that none of the bandits ever washed their clothes. When their clothes got stiff with dirt, they would just put them in a bag and forget about them. Sometimes when we stopped at a cinema to load up on sweets there would be a laundrette nearby, but nobody ever thought to go in and wash their clothes.

"Can that be true?" Wild Karl asked, deadly serious. "The whole month of June has flown by. That's what happens when you're having fun. Wasn't it fun, Maisie?"

"Yes," I replied, just to be polite at first. Then I added, "Loads of fun," and I meant it. It had been more fun than anything else in my life. More fun than I knew anything could be.

"Do we have to spend the night *there*?" Hellie asked. She was giving her newly stolen Barbie doll a Mohican hairstyle. The girl who had owned the Barbie had been so scared she hadn't made a sound. She was the first robbery victim that had stuck in my mind. I'd kept thinking about her after. I had tried to talk about it with Hellie in our tent that night, but she felt no mercy.

"That girl needs to learn that if you look like a Barbie doll with big blue eyes and no mind of your own, you're definitely going to get robbed. Let her learn to get some attitude!" Hellie had fumed.

Is that what I'm like? I had wondered to myself as I lay in my sleeping bag that night. *Big eyes and no mind of my own? At first maybe, but now…*

"Come on, Hilda, we don't need to stay overnight. We could just say hi," Hellie continued. She sprayed a heavy layer of hairspray on the Barbie doll's head. "The boss will just sit there all night reminiscing about old times, and then we'll have to listen to him going on about it all the way to the Summer Shindig. Sorry, but somebody's got to put their foot down. Otherwise it's the same thing every year. Every single year."

I admired Hellie's boldness. I noticed that Wild Karl hadn't shown any sign of anger, just because she'd called him the boss. That's how little it took.

"Where are we headed?" I whispered to Charlie.

"Kate's place," Charlie whispered back. "It's ideal, right along our route."

"Our usual stopping-off place, innit," nodded Golden Pete. "Kate makes us a good square meal."

He rubbed his pancake-filled belly and seemed about to nod off.

I was used to not getting any clear answers. During the journey the only thing I could think about was our next destination after this stop: the bandits' Summer Shindig. That thought made me feel both sad and excited. The Summer Shindig. I had made myself a promise back on the first day after I was kidnapped. I had decided that the Summer Shindig was where I would make my escape.

We stopped on a birch-lined track that led down to a long, shallow lake with birds swimming in it. The heat hit us as we got out of the van and stood on a grassy area with a flagpole flying the Finnish flag. There was a cottage with a large veranda in front. A woman got up from one of the chairs on the veranda and waved. Clearly she knew we were not there for a hold-up. She started running down the garden path towards us. She lost one of her sandals along the way, but that didn't slow her down. She ran towards Wild Karl, who spread his arms wide. And then, just like that, the woman leaped up into his arms and wrapped herself round him with such force that he lost his balance and fell backwards on to the lawn.

"You chunky monkey," she screeched. "You tubby flubby bubby, you."

"You bony old pony," Wild Karl screeched. "Your legs are as thin as chopsticks."

"And yours are like the towers on a castle," she said. Then she started to wrestle with him, huffing and puffing. For a moment it looked as if Wild Karl was losing, but then I realized he was just pretending. Hilda was unloading the van and took no notice of her husband's predicament.

"Well, then, let's go and eat," the woman said, getting her breath back. "The soup's ready."

She bounced up and held out a hand to Wild Karl, who lay gasping on the ground.

"How do you always know?" Hilda asked her good-naturedly. "I bet you've got spies out there somewhere."

"I can hear that old rust-bucket of yours rattling as soon as you turn off the main road," the woman said. "I've got ears. It gives me time to finish a chapter and put the soup on the hob before you get here."

On the veranda she turned to me and said, "Ah, a summer guest. My name's Kate." She shook my hand. Her grip was like a car crusher. "I'm that guy's big sister."

Wild Karl tidied his braids and looked both sheepish and cheerful.

"Inside, you lot," Kate Robberson said. "I'll dig out your mummified washing. Come along, Pete, you can help me carry it into the laundry room. And no arguing. The rest of you, go and eat. That bean soup will keep you going until next week."

Charlie made a fart noise and rolled his eyes. Hellie laughed.

"And the young bandit had better not think that everybody over thirty is deaf," Kate said, whirling round and grabbing Charlie by the ear.

"Sorry, bad joke," he blurted. She let him go.

Hellie went a bit pale too. She also apologized. She slowed down, waiting for me to catch up.

"Be careful about telling her any stories," Hellie said. "She'll use them against you. She's merciless."

"Angela Heartwell," Charlie hissed.

"What about her?" I asked.

Primrose was crazy about Angela Heartwell's novels. They always featured a romantic, mysterious man who still hadn't found his one true love but kept following tantalizing clues in his search for her.

"Kate IS Angela Heartwell," Hellie said. "She puts everything people tell her into her books!"

"Now that you've frightened the daylights out of this girl, you can come and eat," Kate said. She had crept up behind us without us noticing, even though she was lugging huge bags of laundry. And she'd heard everything.

"We were just chatting," Hellie said in desperation.

"Come on, don't lie," Kate snapped. "You'd better behave, Little Miss Bandit, or I'll hang you from the coat rack by your ears. As you'll remember from last year, I always keep my promises." She uttered her threats in a sing-song voice.

I had met a woman who was even fiercer than the bandit clan.

CHAPTER 10

in which the rules of Chocolate Sixes and Wild Karl's story are revealed

"Soooo…" I began, once the soup bowls had been cleared away. I had been formulating my question to Kate all through the meal but decided to wait until everybody had finished eating. And now, after Wild Karl's fourth helping of bean soup, mealtime was over. "Have you ever been a highway bandit? Before you became a writer?"

I yelped when Hellie and Charlie both kicked me in the shins on either side.

"A highway bandit," Kate said. She burst out laughing. She was just like Wild Karl when she laughed. They both slapped their thighs the same way. "Have I ever been a highway bandit?"

"Yeah, or a corner-shop bandit or a summer-cottage bandit or any other kind of bandit. I haven't been involved very long, so I don't know all the different kinds of bandits there are," I said.

"No, I haven't," Kate said, dabbing the tears of laughter from her eyes. "I don't even have any experiences from my youth to speak of. I can definitely say I haven't stolen anything, unless you count a few juicy stories I've overheard on the bus and put into my novels. I've got everything I need here at home, and a little more besides."

Despite my efforts to stop him, Wild Karl told Kate two stories about me. The first was about how I was stolen. The second described how I planned my signature crime, which had meant we could bring her a whole bag of hard toffees – her favourite sweet. I felt good when Wild Karl praised me. Kate kept glancing at me when Wild Karl was really into his story and acting the part of my terrified parents. Her eyes were as bright as a parrot's. I wasn't sure why she was looking at me.

"How's your latest book going?" Hilda enquired as we started clearing up. "I hope we haven't come at a bad time."

"Oh, you know." Kate sighed. "Same as always. Johnny von Dragondorf has met another scheming redhead in the town square." She turned to me, as if to share a secret. "Johnny always falls for redheads, even though it never turns out well for him. This time I think he'll be even more disappointed than usual. Johnny's going to lose the fortune he inherited from a distant relative in my previous book, *Tears after Evensong*."

"Oh, how awful," Hilda said.

"So you do steal things – just in books," I said, delighted.

Kate slapped her thighs again. "That's true," she laughed. "Hey, you were right, Karlito. This one's sharp! Pale as a sheet of paper, but sharp enough to slice your finger."

After dinner, Kate taught us to play Chocolate Sixes. It's the best game I've ever played. I made sure I wrote down the rules exactly. Here they are.

CHOCOLATE SIXES
Noted down by Maisie

To play, you will need a dice, a bar of chocolate (it should be at room temperature), and as many forks as you have players.

To begin the game, unwrap the chocolate bar, place it on the open wrapper and give each player their own fork.

Start taking turns to roll the dice. The youngest player starts.

The person who rolls a six holds their fork in their weaker hand (not the one they normally use to write with) and starts hacking pieces off the bar of chocolate. Any pieces they can spear on their fork and bring to their mouth, they can eat. You're not allowed to use your hands to help. You must keep your stronger hand behind your back.

(If there is a player who doesn't know how to write and isn't good at using a fork, you can make up a special rule for that person.)

Most important rule: The person eating the chocolate should tease the others by groaning with pleasure and going on about how delicious it is.

Second-most important rule: While the person who rolled a six is eating the chocolate, the other players keep taking turns to roll a six as fast as possible. When the next person gets a six, the first eater has to stop eating IMMEDIATELY and the player who has just got a six gets to attack the chocolate bar with their fork. This player should also groan with pleasure and talk about how delicious the remaining pieces the first person hacked off are.

The game continues until the chocolate is gone or people get bored.

Note on the amount of chocolate: In the first round we got through three bars. One milk chocolate, one dark chocolate and one with whole hazelnuts, which was very filling and hard to spear with a fork because of all the round hazelnuts.

"Are you lot going to spend the night here, Karlito?" Kate asked as we all lay on the floor, stuffed with chocolate.

Hellie tried to raise her head to remind her parents what she had said earlier, but she was fuller than anyone else. She was the best player, just like in every other game. She had a perfect dice-rolling action.

"Yep, we're staying," Wild Karl said. "Great game, that Chocolate Sixes. Just as fiendishly, bandit-ly fun as Yahtzee. Many people think that's a matter of luck, but it's really a game of skill. A fellow can't help it if he's just the best at something, can he?"

Charlie nudged me in the ribs. Obviously Wild Karl had already forgotten that the rest of us shamelessly plotted to lose to him every time.

After the game, Kate said the beds were made up for us upstairs. "Hellie, Pete and Charlie, you can go up into the attic. Karl and Hilda, you can have my bed."

"What about you?" Charlie wondered.

"What about me? Maisie and I can each have a sofa," she said, winking at me.

"We can't take your bed," Hilda said.

"Oh, for goodness' sake, you can sleep in a proper bed once or twice a year," Kate said. "No ifs or buts." Then she switched to a voice filled with fake concern. "Oh, the poor old dear with her bad legs, all alone out here in the woods. And I bet she's going a bit soft in the head, the way she laughs at her own jokes." She let out a good cackle.

The rest of us stood frozen to the spot.

"Go on, you lot," Kate said, now serious. "I often sleep downstairs when I'm finishing up a book, so I can get up and go out for some fresh air. It's not just because you're here. You're not that special." Then she cackled again.

Kate made me a bedtime cup of tea with three spoons of honey in it. "If you're riding in that van, you have to get used to sweet things," she said.

We sat outside on the patio. It wasn't very chilly yet.

Kate pointed to a small fridge in a corner of the veranda. "That holds a six-month supply of mustard for Karlito," she said. "I can predict almost to the minute when he'll turn up again."

I peeked inside the fridge. It was completely filled with the same brand of mustard I'd seen the Robbersons eating before. Satisfied, Kate leaned back in her chair and tucked a blanket over her legs. We sat in silence for some time.

Then she said, "You shouldn't get too used to the bandit life." She fixed me with a stern look and I felt as if I'd shrunk to the size of a worm in my chair.

"Are you trying to say I'm not cut out for robbing?" I asked. "If I was completely useless, they would've dropped me off at a petrol station somewhere by now." I was so upset I leaped up to seem a bit taller.

"I can believe that!" Kate cackled. Then she grew serious

again. "What I'm trying to say is you don't get the whole picture in summer. The bandit lifestyle is no fun in winter. The van gets stuck in the snow and even when they stay in my other cottage, it's freezing cold. There's no one out and about on the country roads in January."

"I can handle it," I claimed, although I knew very well I'd be back at home when the autumn rains started.

That was an unwelcome thought.

"Karlito can handle it because he chose that life," Kate continued. "Hilda, I don't know about. Maybe she wants to make him and the kids happy."

"They can handle anything!" I said in the family's defence. "You don't know because you're not there. You don't know what it's like when the van skids to a stop and they leap out with a roar." I stood on the veranda and waved my hand around as if I had a fearsome bandit sword.

"Karlito – I mean Wild Karl – hasn't always been a bandit chief," Kate said. "And soon he won't remember what things were like before."

I sat down as Kate began telling me Wild Karl's story.

"Many years ago, up until Charlie was a toddler and Hellie was five years old, Karlito worked in a car factory," she began.

"I don't believe you," I said. I couldn't imagine the Robbersons' dad in blue dungarees, marching off to a factory as the whistle blew.

"Well, he did," Kate replied. "It was one of the factories in eastern Finland, when there were quite a few of them. Karl thought they made the best, most robust cars in the world. He said he had total faith in those cars because he'd had a hand in making every single part. Karl was extremely good at his job. He knew how to do nearly every task at the factory. In the end he inspected the cars to make sure everything about them was just right. Pete was his best mate, ever since they started working there at the same time. Hilda and the children would watch from the window as Karl would come home from work with Pete. Pete lived on his own but in the same block of flats, and he often came over to their place for dinner. It was an ordinary Finnish block of flats with balconies, where people would put up a red plastic star in their window at Christmas…"

Dusk had finally fallen as Kate told the story. The brief darkness in the light summer night. Her voice was quieter now.

"The news came right around Christmas," she continued. "The factory was to close. The company was moving its manufacturing to some other country where it was cheaper. They said those who wanted could stay on for a little while making mobile phone cases or try to find jobs as metalworkers in another factory. But Karl didn't want to. He only wanted to work on the best, most robust cars he'd worked on his whole life. On one of the last days before Christmas they drew up their plan. I went over there the day after Christmas, but they had gone. The door was open just a crack. The star was in the window, the children's toys were still in their room, clothes still in the wardrobe. But they had left. I thought I'd never see them again. But then, less than six months later at the start of summer, they turned up here in their van."

I tried to imagine the Robbersons' life during that first year. How they would have spent their first night in the bandit van, just like I did. How Hellie and Charlie must have missed their toys and their friends until gradually they began to forget. Until Hellie became an unbeatable super-bandit.

"Karlito didn't dare to come and visit at first because he thought I'd be angry," Kate said. "But how could I be angry at him for wanting to fulfil his dream?" She got up so briskly that her blanket fell to the floor. "Shall we go inside? It's getting chilly," she said.

I closed my eyes and imagined a block of flats with an empty parking space in front. A red Christmas star hung in one window, but there was no one at home.

CHAPTER 11

in which they finally reach the Summer Shindig

"At last," Hellie yelled as she bounced around the kitchen. "At last, at last, at last! We're going at last!"

It was six o'clock in the morning. It felt like Kate and I had only fallen asleep an hour ago. Then something astonishing happened. Hellie made breakfast.

I've never seen anyone make breakfast so fast. She cracked eggs into a bowl with one hand while filling the coffee maker with the other. Then she whisked the eggs while she put bread slices in the toaster. She danced round the kitchen so energetically there seemed to be motion lines swirling behind her.

"Wakey wakey," she trilled, leaping on to a chair and then the table to bang on the ceiling with a saucepan. "Wake up, robbers and bandits, wake up! Estimated time to departure is forty-five minutes."

"Isn't it nice to have a proper kitchen?" Kate said to Hellie. She clipped her hair back as she spoke. This morning Kate just seemed more relaxed, less fierce. As she spoke to Hellie, I suddenly recalled what we were talking about before we went to bed. Wild Karl's past. And Hellie and Charlie's childhood and their toys, which were just left on the floor of their room one day.

"Yep," Hellie said as she pulled a pile of bacon out of the fridge and put it in the pan along with the scrambled eggs. I was amazed at how she seemed to know where everything was. "It helps us get OUT OF HERE quicker!"

Then she banged on the ceiling once more. This time she used so much force it left a mark.

"That girl's got a good voice," Wild Karl said as he came downstairs. "She'll make a fine bandit chief some day."

"I want to be a bandit chief," Charlie said. He slipped past his father on the stairs.

"You can both be chiefs," Wild Karl said. "So long as you don't steal from each other, everything will be fine."

We ate a hearty bandit breakfast, with eggs and bacon and meatballs. Of course, Wild Karl put everything on top of crispbread with a huge stripe of mustard.

Once we'd eaten, the van was loaded in minutes. "See you when it gets cold," he said and planted a kiss on Kate's cheek.

"See you then!" Kate said. "Be the fiercest you can be."

Then she gave another of her cackles and waved goodbye to us as the bandit van's tyres squealed and we drove off.

"We have to rob at least one car before the Summer Shindig," Charlie said. "I haven't got my own knife yet, and I'm going to be ten this autumn. A bandit ought to have a knife."

"Didn't Kate say anything to you?" Hilda asked, then performed a perfect handbrake turn on to the main road. We clung to the door handles to avoid being flung against the sides of the van. "She told me she'd put some presents for you under the seats. Some Summer Shindig presents, but I guess you can open them now."

We dug around underneath the seats. Charlie found his first. Then Hellie. She looked at me as if I was a fool.

"How come you're not looking for yours?" she asked. "Sometimes it seems like you haven't learned a thing. OF COURSE there's a parcel for you as well."

I felt the underside of the bench seat, and there was a little package fastened with tape. It had a ribbon tied round it and a little card that said *Maisie* in lovely handwriting. When had Kate managed to wrap that up and hide it? We'd been up all night together and she got up after me. It seemed that Hellie – who was perfect at everything – wasn't the only exceptional member of the Robberson family. Charlie had already opened his package. Inside was a fine knife with a grey steel blade.

"Wow, a carbon-steel knife," Hellie said. "That will last a

lifetime, as long as you don't do anything stupid."

She tore open her own present. "A butterfly knife," she said appreciatively. Its blade was concealed inside the two halves of the handle. When you folded the handle back, the halves formed a practical grip.

"A nice additional knife for special occasions," Hellie said as she practised opening it with figure-of-eight motions. After a few moments' practice she looked like a Japanese samurai.

"Boss, your sister sure has got good taste in knives," Golden Pete said, impressed.

Quickly, before the others started watching me, I opened my present. I loosened the tape carefully without making a noise. I had learned that from spending years with a jealous older sister. There was my own knife, in a pale-coloured leather sheath. It had a wooden handle and the most beautiful blade in the world. It was sharpened on both sides and had a pattern of flowers and winding vines.

"A *pretty* knife," snorted Hellie. "You ought to wrap some tape around the handle. Wood can slip out of your hand easily."

"Now we're ready for the Summer Shindig," Wild Karl said.

I had thought the bandits' Summer Shindig would be held at some remote campsite far from anyone else, but I was totally wrong. The festival site was a huge sports ground behind a shopping mall. A sign above the entrance read NETWORK MARKETING OF FINLAND SUMMER CONFERENCE. The words were hand-painted on a white bed sheet. Nobody was posted at the entrance to check who drove in. Even so, my hair stood on end with tension.

"Excellent," Wild Karl enthused. "If I lived here and saw that sign, I'd steer well clear."

We were still at the entrance. The campervan in front of us was trying to manoeuvre through the gates. Hilda revved her engine to strike fear into the driver and get them to move.

"Hey, we're not network marketing people," Charlie exclaimed as our bandit van drove in.

"No, neither are we accountants," Hilda said, sticking her tongue out in concentration as she zigzagged to the best parking spot.

"They had to change it from last year, innit, when all sorts of folk turned up looking for 'tax-efficient asset planning' or whatever the sign read," Golden Pete said.

From his careful pronunciation, I could tell that it pained Golden Pete to say that phrase.

"If they have a different sign every year, how can we be sure whether or not these actually are network marketers?" Charlie asked.

"Just take a look, darling," Hilda said gently. "Do these people look like network marketers?" We peered through the side door, then climbed out. At least thirty vans and campervans were parked on the vast, sandy ground. Groups of bandits bustled around each one, putting out garden chairs and setting up plastic marquees. The toughest-looking ones had brought their own barriers, which they were manoeuvring into place to surround their pitch. Those who had finished setting up camp had settled into their chairs to watch the others.

I had never seen a collection of vehicles like it. One had flames painted on every surface. Another had a stepladder bolted to its side, leading up to its roof, and several people seemed more interested in climbing up it than setting up their own camps. Another van had an enormous pair of pliers tied to its roof rack.

"They say you can cut open any metal fence with those," Charlie said. He had been snooping around the van with the pliers until a giant bald-headed man shooed him away.

"Idiots," Hellie snorted. "Anything goes with the country bumpkins from out east these days. Those bolt-cutters are totally illegal. With them on the roof, they're basically calling out to the cops to come after them. No, little bro, it's like this. A proper bandit van is completely unremarkable—" At this point she pulled on a chain to unfurl the pirate flag in the roof vent. "Elegant—" She thumped the side of the van. "And powerful enough to get away. You don't need anything else. Anything else is just a sign of a lack of self-respect."

Whatever Hellie said, the rows of Barbie dolls hanging by their necks in the side windows did lend our van some street cred.

"All right, we've got the annual general meeting coming up tonight," Wild Karl said when he returned to the van. He was holding a greasy-looking paper in one hand and a meat pasty in the other, which he was eating absent-mindedly. The jacket he'd been saving for this special occasion was already starting to look a bit grubby.

"Shocking," he said as he read the paper. He plopped down into a chair next to the van with such force, he was lucky it didn't collapse. "Outrageous! The Farnabys are getting too big for their boots. Listen to this, Hilda. They've invited the Charmers as keynote speakers. The Crazy Charmers. Of all the possible clans! Their old man couldn't catch anybody these days even if he could run! Their youngest lad became an engineer. Oh, for heaven's sake," he fumed, tugging at his braids. "*Robbing today. Contemporary hold-up hacks and the latest techniques.* So this is where things are headed? Is this what we need? Nobody would be at the annual meeting if they didn't already know the basics of robbing!"

"When's B&B?" Hilda asked. "So I know when to start the dough."

"What about G&G?" Charlie piped up. "Is it a two-day event like last year or is there a qualifying round? Is there a lower age limit? Dad, can I be in G&G now if Golden Pete does his MM or whatever it's called? I've been practising for two whole summers, and even Hellie says I'm good at it. Come on, Boss, make a decision!"

"One at a time, you lot!" Wild Karl said. He began reading the festival timetable out loud. The other Robbersons gathered round him. The programme was full of abbreviations that must have been specialist terms in their line of work.

"Welcome to the Summer Shindig," said a woman passing by our pitch. She wore a short summer dress and a leather waistcoat with an F on it. She was carrying a little dog – probably a miniature pinscher – which had four studded collars in different sizes and a matching leather waistcoat with a big white F on it. "Remember the rules: Peace and respect! So nice you could come!"

As the woman walked past, Wild Karl grabbed hold of Hilda round her waist and placed his hand over her mouth to keep her quiet until the woman was out of earshot.

"I wish you'd let me show that Farnaby woman what I think of her," Hilda hissed. She was furious. "I can't listen to her! She's so stuck-up! 'So nice you could come' – as if it was *their* party, their back garden. Do they live here now?"

"You'll thrash her at B&B, then she'll keep her mouth shut until next summer," Wild Karl said. "Focus. Beat them, then we'll teach them about *respect*."

This Summer Shindig was revealing a new side to the Robbersons. I clearly still had a lot to learn.

CHAPTER 12

in which there are plenty of challenges

After the encounter with the Farnaby woman, everybody went off to do their own thing. Wild Karl met with the other bandit chiefs, Hilda spread out her baking things on the folding table and asked Golden Pete to set up a marquee over our pitch, so outsiders couldn't see what she was doing. Hellie stayed with me.

"Let's go over these events," she said helpfully. "The boss finally decided to let Charlie take part in G&G. That stands for Guess and Grab. It's a two-day competition where you have to guess what's in the boot of a car based on just a quick glance. It's judged according to who has the best hold-up strategies and takes particular risks. The boss used to take part, but he always got so worked up in the final that it's better if Charlie has a go instead."

Beneath the marquee, Hilda started kneading her dough. It contained a mixture of rye flour and a large quantity of kidney beans that had been soaked and ground into a paste.

"You kids go for a walk," she said, out of breath from working the dough. "But don't start chatting to anyone and don't make eye contact. Take the walkie-talkie with you. You know the drill."

I waited for Hellie to get ready. She took some things from her rucksack and put them in her pockets for our little excursion around the site. She slid her sheath knife into one of her biker boots. She had added a new loop to her belt for her butterfly knife, ready to grab in a matter of seconds. Hellie also put a can of pepper spray in her pocket. Then she took an impressive length of steel chain and threaded it through her belt loops, like a second belt. While she was tooling up for battle, she also explained the rules of the upcoming competition.

"Hilda's going to do B&B," she said. "It's an annual competition. The name stands for Baking and Battle. The rules were tightened up last year. You can only use edible ingredients in the pies – you're no longer allowed to poison other people. Now the judges also taste the pies and actually award points, which is a big improvement. The competitors used to sneak plaster and coal and all sorts into their pies for their opponents to eat."

Hellie noticed my horrified expression and quickly added, "Baking and Battle is a two-event competition. First, each competitor has to bake a pie. Each pie is divided into as many pieces as there are competitors, usually six to eight, and then there is a piece for the judges as well. This year, points will be awarded for flavour and appearance. Then each competitor eats a piece of all the other competitors' pies, so six to eight pieces. You can't leave anything on your plate, or you're instantly disqualified."

As I was taking notes and trying to keep up with Hellie, my pencil lead snapped.

"The second round of the competition is wrestling," she continued. "Everybody takes on everybody else in turns, one-on-one. Right after the pie-eating. Points are awarded as in Olympic wrestling. Then the scores from the pie round are added to the wrestling scores. The person with the highest total is declared that year's B&B champion and can put their title on the side of their van if they want."

I scanned around all the vehicles I could see from where I was sitting.

"I don't see the title on any of the vans," I said.

"Of course not," Hellie snorted. "Hilda wins every year. One year she had her arm in a sling and still won. It's a messy, violent, brilliant competition! You've got to see it. Tomorrow at three."

"Do you want to take part when you grow up?" I asked.

Hellie gave me the same look I remembered from our first day together. I could feel my facial muscles start to tremble under her fiery gaze. She quickly softened when she realized how clueless I was about the whole thing.

"Me, bake a pie?" she scoffed. "Come *on*."

When Hellie was fully equipped at last, she took me on a tour. The Farnaby clan's pitch, behind the barrier, was especially scary. It was the biggest and noisiest one in the whole place. Another van full of young people drove up. A section of the barrier was moved aside and then returned to its place lightning quick as soon as the van entered their compound.

"They're totally overrated," Hellie said, sucking on a liquorice lolly, one of the few remaining ones from the kiosk heist. We walked towards the fence. The Farnabys' little dog ran up to the other side and yapped at us. Despite the hot weather, it was still dressed in its monogrammed leather waistcoat.

"The Farnabys have their big chief, but that's it. He's the guy that Wild Karl and Golden Pete worship above all else," she explained. "But he can't even come down here any more. I guess he's in some hospital ward or maybe even dead, but nobody's allowed to talk about it."

The dog was still barking at us, so Hellie chucked her

lolly stick at it. The dog pounced on the stick. Just then a tent flap opened and an older man came out. He wasn't wearing a shirt, just an open waistcoat with an F on it and a pair of shorts.

"What are you two gawping at?" he demanded. He picked up the dog under one arm and sniffed the lolly stick to make sure it wasn't poisoned.

"Just looking around," Hellie said.

"Well, now you've looked, and you know you're in the wrong place. The Farnabys only give one warning," he said, aiming a finger at us like a gun.

He gave the dog a squeeze and took it into the tent.

"He's their new second-in-command," Hellie said. "Their boss is in the main tent. He's the big, bald guy also wearing an 'F' waistcoat. Well, he will be the boss if they ever get that old codger to step down."

"The boss wears the same outfit as the dog," I giggled.

We walked over towards some purple vans that each had a picture of a knife on their rear bumper.

"Better watch out for this lot," Hellie said in a low voice, crunching on the last of her lolly. "The Flying Stilettos. From the west coast. If you ever drive up towards Oulu or Jakobstad, two or three of these vans will materialize out of nowhere."

As we strolled past their pitch, one van's side door opened and an older, frizzy-haired woman scowled at us.

"That's Old Hannah, their commander-in-chief," Hellie whispered. "Lethal kebab pie with a rye crust that sits in your stomach like a pile of bricks. Excellent arm strength. She's the one Hilda needs to beat at B&B. The others don't amount to much."

"How's your mum doing?" Old Hannah asked. "Hope she hasn't wasted away to nothing thanks to your refined ways. I heard you locked some old crone in the boot of her car and then ran blubbing to the police because you were worried she might get upset."

A whole group of men's voices roared with laughter inside the van.

"Oh, Mum? She's over there baking some razor blades into her pies," Hellie said. "Shall I tell her you said hi?"

"Like mother, like daughter – they've both got nasty mouths," Old Hannah remarked to her audience in the van. "Who's the rag doll there?"

"She's the expert we stole," Hellie replied brightly. "You'll just have to wait and see what she can do. Only then it'll be too late for you."

She really shouldn't have said that.

The bandit chiefs' meeting took place in a big circus tent, but there was a large, strong-looking man standing guard at the door.

"I thought people came here to compare reputations and honour," I said after we'd swerved to avoid a man being chucked out of the tent.

"You can't do that to a Beast from the East!" he shouted before charging back inside.

The doorman looked pretty amused.

"Yes, they did," Hellie explained. "In the past, people used to just brag about their own feats and then in the evenings they'd fight. The most exciting thing was stealing items from other groups' pitches. In those days I'm sure we would have competed to get those silly pliers off the roof of that van after dark. The Great Farnaby, the supreme boss back in the '80s, understood how dangerous it was when the different camps came into conflict over silly pranks. So he came up with these events. Some have been dropped, like 'Dare or Die'. Over the years it became too hazardous. Crazy, right? The players always took the dare, but they ended up dying anyway. Instead they introduced some less dangerous events, so now there's B&B and MM."

"MM? What's that? Major Mudfight? Meatball Mayhem?" I guessed.

Hellie tried to keep a straight face but couldn't. "Those would be better events than what we've got now," she said. "It stands for Miniature Models. They have to be made from stolen or found materials – no ready-made parts allowed. MM is Golden Pete's obsession. None of

118

us have seen his model of the bandit van he's got in that cardboard box. Two weeks ago it was nearly finished, just needed to be painted."

"One question," I said. "How do you know it's a model of the bandit van?"

"I just know," she said with a wink.

CHAPTER 13
in which the games begin

It was a restless night. We pitched the dome tent right next to the van, partly sheltered under the marquee. The tent pegs wouldn't stay in the sandy ground, so we had to figure out other ways to secure the ropes. Charlie said they'd already been briefed on the task for the G&G elimination round. It involved guessing the contents of a car boot, same as last year. In the morning they would get ten seconds after the boot was opened to guess what was inside and then estimate how much they'd be able to shift into a bandit van within two minutes. The target vehicle had been set out that evening, so people could calculate the boot capacity and size of the opening ahead of the competition.

"They don't want anybody to sleep tonight," Charlie grumbled. "Nobody ever remembers this bit of the shindig, they just go on about how much fun they had."

"You all go to sleep," Golden Pete said, glancing around as night fell. "I'm stayin' up to keep an eye out, make sure nobody comes a-trespassin', innit. Last year Lenny from the Beasts from the East made himself a mighty fine model. An old-school diesel train it was. Now we all agreed this was a friendly competition. But then the night before the judging, somebody sneaks in and smashes the front of it – smashes it right in. Lenny's out of the running and the trophy goes to Antony Charmer. Full of himself, that fella. The way he carried on, it wasn't hard to guess who smashed up Lenny's train."

"The Farnabys and Charmers have been cosying up too much for my liking," Wild Karl said. "It's not good for the rest of us."

Hellie and I tried to get to sleep, but we could hear Charlie mumbling from his sleeping bag next to us. "A dry rug, one to two kilos, twenty seconds transfer time, wet rug, weight times four, transfer time times two."

"Quiet now," Hellie ordered. "It always seems like normal people lose their minds when they're here."

"It's easy for you – you've got it all already," Charlie said, sitting up in his sleeping bag. "Dad's always saying, 'Hellie's going to be a bandit chief, Hellie's going to make such a great chief' – but he never says anything about me. I need to win at G&G, otherwise for the rest of the summer

I'm going to hear, 'Should've known Charlie can't think for himself, he's a gentleman robber'. If I hear that one more time, I'm going to smash something with a hammer!"

"Sorry," Hellie said, looking sheepish. "I didn't know you felt that way."

"Goodnight," Charlie said gloomily. And he turned his back to us.

I awoke to an empty tent. I'd had a restless night, startling at the slightest sound. I was certain the Farnabys and the Beasts from the East were sneaking up on our tent to club us all to death.

When I got up, the Robbersons had already eaten their bandit breakfast. I saw Charlie wave goodbye as he headed off to the preliminary G&G round in one of the big tents.

"Tinned breakfast," Wild Karl said as he handed me a tin opener. "Hilda's getting herself ready. Her name was selected for the first wrestling match this morning. She's up against Mia Levander, so it should be a walkover. Mia's a puny little thing, not built for it."

"No such thing as a walkover, Boss," Golden Pete said. He'd stayed awake all night to protect us. "Got to treat each match like it's the only one. Plenty of folk come a cropper when they think they've got a victory in the bag. The ones up against Charlie are set to find that out soon enough."

After breakfast (tinned peaches, tinned meatballs and a couple of sardines) we went to watch the pies being judged for the first B&B event before they were divided up and eaten. The weather was so nice the event had been moved outdoors.

"Eating time is five minutes per piece," a voice said over the loudspeaker. "Points will be deducted for each minute of additional time. More than ten minutes will lead to disqualification."

The six competitors were lined up behind their pies, already wearing their wrestling leotards. They all looked really fierce. Hilda was one of the most intimidating with her stripy leotard and her hair in a bun. Old Hannah from the Flying Stilettos made a face when she saw Hilda. I assumed that the small, dark-haired woman in a black leotard was Hilda's first opponent, Mia Levander. The Beasts from the East were represented by a woman who looked like she was more of an expert on pies than wrestling. The Farnabys were sending Hilda's arch-enemy into the ring: young Tula Farnaby. Her outfit was red and featured their clan's emblem: a flame with a white 'F'. Tula waved confidently from the stage and blew a kiss to her husband, who was holding their mascot, the waistcoat-wearing dog. The dog was panting in the heat.

"Nobody knows who that is," Hellie said, pointing to a woman in green with sweatbands round her wrists. "I heard they only turned up last night. A new crew, apparently from the islands or Åland. But they seem to know their stuff and don't go round flapping their mouths."

"… And representing the Offshore Raiders, Anna-Katri Mikkonen, also known as AK," the announcer said. The woman in green raised her hand and waved to everyone in the audience. Her eyes were clear and penetrating, without fear.

"Good physical control," Hellie said. "You can tell. That one's going to be a challenge for Hilda."

It was time for the pie-eating. I watched as Hilda sized up the pieces piled in front of her and began to eat. Quickly, efficiently, looking out into the distance. Five huge pieces of pie. One of them would have made a decent lunch on its own. I couldn't understand how anyone could cram that much food in their belly.

"She uses visualization techniques to train. Guess who she imagines when she's eating." Hellie giggled. "In a minute she's going to ask for a stripe of mustard on top."

Mia Levander, one of the competitors, gagged on a bite of pie.

"Spitting, two-point penalty," said the voice over the loudspeaker. The audience gasped. People had come from the other tents to watch the pie-eating. Only those who had been at the first G&G rounds were elsewhere.

"Excellent," Hellie said. "Hilda's going to win by

default soon."

The Beasts from the East competitor also started to gag. Her piece looked the same as Levander's. It was the lightest-coloured one, with an innocent leaf design on top.

Golden Pete made his way over to us. "Somebody didn't go and put sand in it, did they?" he said, worried. "I thought they kept an eye on things in the judges' tent. Sand would be a low-down, dirty trick, against all the rules."

"Not sand," Hellie said, deep in thought. I could tell the gears were whirring inside her head. "It's salt. Pepper would be visible – that's an old trick. The Beasts tried it two years ago. Salt, though. Big points for AK there. The ones who can manage to get it down will need to drink loads of water, and that's no good for wrestling."

I saw Hilda pick up her piece of the light-coloured pie and take a bite. From the way her eyebrow twitched I could sense how salty the pie must be. But she took another bite. On the third bite, halfway through the piece, she turned to her opponent from the Offshore Raiders and gave a big smile.

It was the hottest part of the afternoon and the final B&B round was approaching. Hilda had beaten Mia Levander in their pairing. Mia looked unwell right from the start of the match. Afterwards, she went behind the maintenance trailer to throw up a heroic amount of salty pie. But the other matches continued. Old Hannah had pinned down the woman from the Beasts from the East. The longest, most exciting match was the test of strength between the newcomer AK and the young Farnaby. Due to numerous time outs, their first-round match was still in progress long after the others had been decided.

"AK's trying to take her down," Hellie said. "Wants to pin her with the first takedown if she can. You've got to hang on to her so she can't get the upper hand. Hopefully Hilda is watching this."

Hilda was watching, with her teeth clenched and her arms crossed. Wild Karl tried to massage her shoulders and offer her a water bottle, but she shooed him away. She seemed to have her own game plan.

"Charlie's doing a bang-up job in the G&G heats. What'd I tell yer?" Golden Pete whispered when he reappeared next to me. "He's leading on points right now. They're taking a break – well, more like a fistfight broke out over something the judges did. Just yer regular stuff."

"OK, there it is," Hellie said as AK of the Offshore Raiders finally got a decent hold that left her opponent no wiggle room. The match was over. The winner raised her arm briefly and glanced out at the audience. She resembled a slightly older version of Hellie.

Hilda was lucky in the second-round draw. She was paired against Tula Farnaby, who was tired from her long

126

first-round match. It was over quickly. Hardly anyone watched Hilda wrestle. Most of the spectators flocked to the opposite side to see how the mysterious newcomer AK Mikkonen performed against Old Hannah. AK did so well that she shortened the whole tournament. The Beasts from the East participant got a bye into the next round thanks to Mia Levander's exit, so she came over to watch Old Hannah and AK wrestle. After seeing AK in action, halfway through the match she went over to the judges and told them she was withdrawing from the competition.

"I wonder if any of them have ever actually felt fear before," Hellie mused over a glass of squash as we waited for the final match to start. "Sometimes it seems like bandits are only capable of thinking about one thing at a time."

We were back at our camping pitch, soaking up the sun and eating gummy rats straight from the bag. We had topped up our stock after our visit to Kate. Passers-by looked on enviously – and rightly so; gummy rats, squash and sunshine were the perfect combination.

"AK is a good wrestler," Hellie said. "But it's not just about baking and wrestling, it's about the younger generation of bandits! The Raiders are a young crew with their own approach and very little regard for the old boundaries."

Boundaries, I wrote in my diary. There was a huge

amount to learn about robbing.

"It's awesome!" Hellie chuckled as she lowered a huge green and black rat into her mouth by its tail. "A little action, some surprises. About time too!"

"You kids will come to the dining tent as soon as the final is over, won't yer?" Golden Pete said. He climbed in the van and fetched his grey cardboard box. "I'm goin' to get ready. MM is starting soon, and there's no rule against you coming to cheer me on neither. It'll feel good to take the title away from that Charmer, if there's any justice in this world, innit."

"Due to a dispute about the final G&G rankings, the scores will be recalculated," a voice said over the loudspeaker. "The G&G scores will be recalculated by the independent panel of B&B experts. As a result, the B&B final will be postponed for one hour. Competing in the final are AK Mikkonen of the Offshore Raiders and the reigning champion Hilda Robberson. That's the B&B final on Mat Number One, exactly one hour from now."

"Time out," Wild Karl said as he entered the tent. He looked sweaty. His T-shirt had damp patches in the armpits, and his captain's coat was tied round his waist. "This has never happened before! They're changing the rules! You can't just announce changes like that. You have to have a general meeting with all the chiefs first. Read the manual! The Farnabys are getting too big for their boots!"

"It'll be a dull final," Hellie said. "Pure wrestling skill. They'll have had time to digest their pie. Hilda will have a harder time – the salt will just make her feel worse with this waiting. Crooked judges, that's what I say. Of course, they tasted those pies so they know about the salt."

Hilda returned to our van and got into the driving seat. She slammed the door shut. It was clear she was concentrating and we shouldn't speak to her.

"I don't want to hang about here. Let's go and check out the town," Hellie said. "What else has it got to offer besides a sports field?"

"Take the walkie-talkie," Wild Karl said, chucking it to us.

"Yeah, yeah, Boss," Hellie said as she caught it.

As we left the Summer Shindig site, I turned and looked at the NETWORK MARKETING OF FINLAND SUMMER CONFERENCE sign fluttering in the breeze. Even at first glance, the event at the sports ground looked like something completely different. Bandits in dark clothing lounged by their vans. G&G competitors could be heard fighting in their tent. The Farnabys' tiny guard dog tried to bark, but the sound came out like a little shriek.

We turned left on to the main street. It was pretty empty. There was a petrol station. A sign at the end of a gravel track pointed to a health centre.

"Isn't the shindig's security a bit weak?" I wondered.

"Has anybody ever thought what would happen if someone noticed what was really going on and everybody got arrested?"

"Like I said, most bandits are REALLY not that smart," Hellie replied. She bent down to do up her bootlaces in the shade of the petrol station canopy. "They think if the camp looks scary enough, outsiders won't venture in." Then she brightened. "Hey, you've never robbed a petrol station, have you?" She gestured for me to follow her. We tiptoed right up to the café. "Tell me where you would start if you were going to do a hold-up," she instructed. "What factors should you take into account if you were going to walk through that door a couple of minutes from now and clear out all the sweets they've got?"

I scanned the area. "Well, there are CCTV cameras pointing at the entrance. The staff door leads to the back room, and the double doors lead to the outdoor seating area. One of them is stuck open," I observed.

"Not bad. You ought to try G&G," she beamed.

At that very moment my gaze landed on a familiar figure. I had to look three times for it to sink in. Queuing at the till, dressed in his summer clothes, was my father, Jon Vainisto.

CHAPTER 14

in which everything goes wrong, leading to a car chase

I ducked below the window so Dad wouldn't see me. He was showing my photo to the assistant at the petrol-station café. The assistant gestured in the direction of the sports ground. A short walk over there and Dad would find the Robbersons' van. He looked annoyed, overheated, the way he usually looked when he wanted to be somewhere else.

After my initial shock, I wasn't that surprised to see Dad. It was easy to track my movements. He just had to follow the trail of sweets by looking at the cinema chain account. The latest batch was from the nearest city two days ago. Too close. I was getting careless.

In the first weeks I had often imagined how it would feel if Mum and Dad came to rescue me. I thought it would feel good. Now it didn't feel like anything. Or, if

I'm honest, it felt like a let-down.

"Your dad's a pretty good detective," Hellie said. I had nearly forgotten she was there. I was impressed that she recognized him – she had only seen him briefly from the window of the bandit van.

Through the window, I saw Dad rub his forehead. He decided to buy a coffee and an ice cream. Fortunately he sat down near the till and not by the window, so we didn't have to leave. He leafed through a newspaper, not noticing that the daughter he was searching for was staring at him just a few metres away. I saw that his face was red.

Of course, he had come after me now that he was being pressed for money. Up to that point it was fine that I was missing, but when Jon Vainisto started losing money, that was the last straw. That must be why he was here. Not because of me.

"Well?" Hellie asked. "What shall we do?" She sprang over to the doors. "You could just go in and I could tell the others that you've run away. True, nobody gets away from me if I don't want to let them go, but I could lie and get the boss to believe me."

"What?" I asked in amazement. It hadn't even occurred to me that Hellie might let me go. "Wild Karl would be furious if I ran away. I'm useful to you!" Suddenly I was almost begging her to let me go back with her.

"Your choice," Hellie said with a shrug. "I'm just saying

you could leave. It gets pretty boring after the Summer Shindig. More of the same robbing and a few summer cottage gigs and stuff. Maybe a little blackmail. Couple of car chases. Same old, same old."

A family with two small children came out. The children were licking ice creams. The heat was melting the little boy's down his hand. All I had to do was step inside. Then I knew.

"You're lying," I exclaimed. "You're trying to trick me, you dirty rat! You're loving this!"

I expected her to burst out laughing or pull a face.

"Of course I am," she said in satisfaction. "Just wanted to see if you were really one of us." She ducked under the windows on the other side of the door and set off towards the camp. I followed her.

We ran along a short stretch of the main road to the sports ground. On the way Hellie told me of her plan to get the other Robbersons and Golden Pete to leave in the middle of the Summer Shindig.

"Hilda will be annoyed to miss the final," she said. "But with her track record she'd win it again this year. Next year is a different story. That AK is a real contender."

To my surprise, I was able to jog along without getting out of breath while also discussing the plan. We agreed that Charlie and Golden Pete would be the hardest to persuade. Charlie was leading on points in his event. Poor Pete's model competition was only just getting under way, and he had stayed up all night guarding his model and us.

"Worst-case scenario, we might have to collect Golden Pete from a railway station somewhere," Hellie said. "We can't wait. We've got a fifteen-minute head start at most."

Then the walkie-talkie crackled. Hellie hurried to get it out of her hidden pocket. We could hear Hilda's voice, but there was too much static to make out her words.

"Something's wrong," she said. "Otherwise they wouldn't contact us."

We broke into a sprint.

When we got back to the sports park, everything had changed. The camp was in total chaos. The bandits who had been watching the competitions had gone back to their own vehicles. The Robbersons' engine was running and Hilda was really revving it. Our camping gear had vanished. Everybody who had been in the two main tents was out on the sandy pitch. A huge commotion was in progress. Everyone was squabbling. Wild Karl was in the middle of it all, shouting louder than anyone. People were packing their things into the other vehicles as well. The Farnabys made a huge racket as they stacked up their barrier. Old Hannah from the Flying Stilettos stood on the ladder on the side of their van and shouted orders.

Tents were torn down, tables were folded up and everyone was running around. People were shooting dirty looks in the direction of the Robbersons' van. It looked as if the others were getting ready to chase us.

"Hurry up," Charlie shouted, hanging on to the Flinger. "We've got to get out of here!"

What on earth had happened in such a short time? Had the Robbersons been so successful in the competitions that the other bandits voted to revolt? What had Wild Karl been careless enough to brag about?

"Girls, stay where you are," Hilda shouted to us. She was still wearing her wrestling gear. She rolled down her window and leaned out, keeping her foot on the gas and one hand on the steering wheel, ready to leave.

The commotion outside the main tents got worse. People in the crowd clenched their fists and their grumbling turned to outrage. When some bandits reached for their knives, Wild Karl decided to make a run for it.

"Just you try it!" he roared. With five giant leaps he reached the van. "Just you try, you rotten scoundrels!"

At that point Wild Karl grabbed the Flinger after Charlie and leaped into the front passenger seat. Charlie helped him get inside. The front door slammed shut, but his voice still carried outside. "Amateurs! Snot-nosed brats!"

The bandit van raced towards us. The side door opened. All the while, Wild Karl kept raging: "Lego pirates are more frightening than you lot!"

Before I could even blink, Golden Pete grabbed hold of my shirt and lifted me into the van. Hellie hopped in on her own.

"Buckle up. Now we'll see what this baby can do," Hilda said cheerfully. The promise of a car chase seemed to have made her forget about missing the wrestling final. "Fingers crossed there aren't any speed cameras or police!"

"Turn right, Hilda! Right!" Hellie and I both yelled, but she had already turned left.

With a great deal of noise and cursing, we drove past the petrol station where Jon Vainisto, having finished his ice cream, was just leaving. I saw his expression change as we zoomed past. From the rear window I saw him stumble and break into a run towards his car. Things could not get any worse.

"Well, now we've got Maisie's search party on our tail, along with the police and most of Finland's highway robbers," Hellie said calmly. "Nice little challenge." She fumbled for the atlas, then curled up to leaf through it. It was all the rest of us could do to stay in our seats as Hilda tore through red lights to reach the motorway.

"Hideouts," Hilda barked. "Look under H. Within a hundred-kilometre radius of here, on a minor road."

"I'm on it," Hellie said.

"I can report that only Maisie's dad and a police car are

tailing us," Charlie noted. He sounded pleased. "The vans from the Summer Shindig won't get beyond the gravel road. They've all got some serious tyre damage."

Without taking her eyes off the atlas, Hellie raised her hand and Charlie gave her a high five.

"That's my boy," Wild Karl shouted. "A perfect signature crime!" He put his hand over his heart and turned to Hilda. Beaming with pride, he said, "Our Charlie is growing up! What smart kids! Soon they'll have their own van and we'll be able to read in the paper about all the things they get up to!"

"I still would've rather won the G&G final," Charlie said in a small voice.

"Let's deal with this first," Hilda said, gritting her teeth. "Hang on, everybody!"

With squealing tyres, the bandit van skidded on to the motorway. A police siren sounded in the distance.

"You're not going to like this," Hellie announced. "The nearest hideout is Kate's place. The next closest is another fifty kilometres north, and there are too many main roads nearby."

They weighed up the options.

"Kate's it is then," Wild Karl said. "I guess she'll take us in again."

Hilda pressed even harder on the gas pedal. I didn't think the van had any more oomph in it, but it did.

"So what actually happened?" Hellie asked. "Did something go wrong in the competitions? Did Charlie make it into the G&G final?"

"Yeah, I did," Charlie said. "While they were trying to work out who would be in the final, I thought it was time to try out my new knife on their tyres. They kept arguing about the scores, even though somebody had already made a complaint about the judging. At that point I figured it was all going to go wrong anyway. The one time I really put some effort into something, it still doesn't turn out."

"So what was the big fight about?" I wanted to know.

Charlie's miserable expression made me feel sorry for him, but I also had a burning desire to find out what had happened.

Golden Pete shook his head. "It was me who threw a spanner in the works," he said. "It all started with those blasted mouse farts. But how was I to know? I sure didn't do it on purpose, no, sir. It was an accident. I mean, them boxes look just alike."

"Mouse farts," Wild Karl said glumly. "Nothing good ever comes of them."

I started giggling uncontrollably. The atmosphere was so tense, yet it was impossible to get any sense out of these guys.

"I did tell you to burn that box," Hilda said grimly. "Now you see what happens."

"What are you talking about?" I said, wiping my eyes. My belly was still shaking with laughter – laughter and tension and surprise.

"Show her," Hellie said to Golden Pete.

Golden Pete took a large cardboard box down from the rack above the back seat. It was the same box he had taken over to the dining tent. He handed it to me.

"Mouse farts. When you're around bandits you can't use 'em, can't show 'em, always a big to-do," he said.

I opened the box and peeked inside. It was full of 100- and 500-euro notes in big bundles secured with red rubber bands. The bundles were as thick as my wrist. Thousands upon thousands of euros. Several hundred thousand, it looked like.

"Back in the old days these used to have a picture of a fella on 'em," Golden Pete explained, taking one banknote from a bundle. "You could fold it so his ear looked like a mouse. When we was bored we'd do it for fun. But these new ones are worse. They don't even work. For making mice, I mean."

"That's why they're mouse farts," Wild Karl said. "Good for lighting fires, but cardboard boxes are even better."

"We found them when we spent the night in an abandoned house," Charlie said, perking up a bit. "They were up in the attic underneath an old wall hanging. We thought we might as well take them. But they've turned out to be more of a nuisance than anything."

"Mouse farts – they're nothing but trouble. Always the same," Golden Pete grumped. "I thought this was the box my model van was in, see, and I didn't realize until I was out there. Well, a couple of those bundles fell on to the ground, and that's when the whole palaver started."

"They went mad, the lot of them," Wild Karl said. "They said they wanted a cut. They'd heard we'd had more than our fair share of good heists recently, and they said it wasn't right. I told them Maisie's ideas are ours and they should come up with their own. We're no do-gooders."

Hellie burst out laughing. Tears started streaming down her cheeks. She had a very odd sense of humour.

"Nope," she said once she was able to speak. "We're more like do-badders."

We turned on to the winding track that led to Kate's cottage just before a string of police cars came racing from the opposite direction – towards the bandits' Summer Shindig.

CHAPTER 15

in which pros and cons - and a disguise - are weighed up

The bandit van screeched up to Kate's cottage. She rushed out, looking worried. "What is it? Has somebody sliced their leg open? Or something worse?"

I felt relieved to see her.

Everyone in the van had been completely silent for the last few minutes on the gravel road. The oncoming police cars had made us all realize we were just a heartbeat away from getting caught. This was not a game, even though that was how I'd started thinking of my summer holidays.

Hilda parked the van and immediately called out to Kate to fetch a tarpaulin. They needed to cover the van in case anyone decided to search the houses and cottages in the area.

"Who's after you?" Kate asked, growing pale. "Should I be worried?" She cast her eyes over each one of us, making sure we were OK.

"They're all after us," Wild Karl said glumly. "The Farnabys and the Charmers and the Levanders. Oh, and the Flying Stilettoes and the Beasts from the East, and whatever the new guys are called. All of them! Everybody who can think of a reason to come after us is after us!"

"Basically every bandit clan you can imagine," Charlie said, giving a nod like an expert.

"And the cops, bringing up the rear," Golden Pete added, shaking his head gloomily. "I reckon this won't end well, innit."

"There's Maisie's dad as well," Hellie said for the sake of completeness, although she knew nobody was paying attention. "Don't forget Jon Vainisto," she repeated. "The rage of an annoyed Manager Mel is limitless. He's the most dangerous of the lot."

Then we ran out of things to say. We had fled here to Kate's place, and now she was supposed to rescue us somehow. Or at least tell us what to do.

Kate tried to lighten the mood. "So a few bandit gangs are cross. That's no big deal," she said. "It was only a matter of time before you upset the rest of them. We've got a real talent for winding up people in this family. You know that, Karlito."

"No, we haven't," Wild Karl insisted as he got out of the van. "Nobody's got any reason to be mad at me.

People don't respect the rules any more. The rule book dates back to the time of the Great Farnaby and—"

"Come off it," Kate interrupted Wild Karl's sermon. "You got on their nerves on purpose. At least have the guts to admit it!"

Kate glanced at me and winked. It seemed as if she was laying the groundwork for another wrestling match.

"Never," Wild Karl roared. "Stop it, Kate! You don't get it. That's not how proper, self-respecting bandits behave. Not the bandits I know." He sat down on the van's step and let his head droop.

Kate stood next to the van, looking uncertain.

"Bandits don't demand other bandits' loot like that. Bandits don't chase after other bandits. This makes no sense," Wild Karl said. He buried his face in his hands. His braids dangled limply.

"I know, Chief," Golden Pete said, crouching next to him. "Right from the start, I had a feeling something weren't right."

"Chasing after us as if we were complete strangers," Wild Karl sobbed. "That's not the way to do things. Not in a world where there are still country roads and freedom and some sort of manners."

"Anyway… Is there a tarpaulin we can use?" Hilda asked.

"I know there's one in the garage," Hellie said.

We went over to open the garage door. Wild Karl clearly needed some time alone.

After we'd got the tarpaulin, Kate made us hot chocolate and warmed up some sweet buns. As we sat and ate, the Summer Shindig began to seem like a distant memory. Wild Karl took a few slurps of hot chocolate and said he was going to bed.

"That brother of mine always wants to go to sleep when things get tough," Kate said. "He was like that even as a little lad."

"I'll go and keep him company," Hilda said gently. "You'll be all right down here, won't you?"

Kate said we could do whatever we liked as long as we weren't noisy. She wanted to finish writing the scene between Johnny von Dragondorf and the scheming redhead in which the handsome hero grows wise to her tricks. Kate started mumbling lines of dialogue. She shut herself in the living room. Soon the sounds of tapping on her keyboard could be heard through the door.

I stayed in the kitchen and started writing a summary of the situation. It was a difficult chore putting these things in writing.

ANALYSIS OF THE ROBBERSONS' SITUATION
Noted down by Maisie

1. The Summer Shindig was called off when a large sum of cash was found in a cardboard box in the Robbersons' van.

2. The Robbersons had discovered the cash in an abandoned house. There is no rightful owner - at least not that anyone knows of.

3. The other bandit clans demanded to have a share of the Robbersons' loot, which the Robbersons would not allow.

4. Possible reasons for the demand:

    a. The other bandits are worse off than the Robbersons and need some money to get through the autumn and winter.

    b. The Robbersons appeared to be boasting when they waved the money around. The demand to share it was a response to that.

    c. The Robbersons had discovered another bandit clan's stash of cash in the abandoned house!!!

5. Consequences of the dispute about cash: the squabble turned into a full-blown argument between the Robbersons and the other bandit clans.

6. Then there was a car chase.

7. The Robbersons managed to get away, thanks to:

    a. Their super-fast packing technique.

    b. Hilda's excellent driving skills.

    c. Charlie's signature crime - he slashed the tyres on the other vans so they couldn't chase after us.

8. During the argument (or straight after), somebody called the police to the Summer Shindig.

9. One or more bandit clan might have been arrested when

they couldn't drive off after us.
10. It's highly likely that the other bandit clans will blame the Robbersons if they get arrested!!!

"You know, it's no use worrying whether you'll be allowed to go to next year's Summer Shindig," I said. "I suspect there won't be one."

And if you see another bandit van, you should hit the gas pedal just as hard as if it was a police car, I thought, but didn't say out loud. The Robbersons' entire life was about to change. I just didn't know whether they realized it yet.

"So who called the cops?" Charlie wondered. He had been reading over my shoulder.

I quickly shut my diary. I didn't want to worry the others, especially Charlie, who was already feeling low after the G&G competition had come to an abrupt end.

"Shall we bet on it? The winner gets a year's supply of sweets," Hellie said slyly. "Or even better: you can have the butterfly knife if you're right."

Charlie seemed interested.

"Don't bother, Charlie," I said. "It was my dad."

We all tiptoed around the cottage until a creak on the stairs alerted us that Wild Karl had woken up from his nap. Everyone gathered in the kitchen. We needed to come up with some sort of plan.

"Can I make a suggestion?" I asked Wild Karl, who was rubbing the sleep from his eyes. They had dark circles under them and he looked pale and weary, as if his sleep had not been restful. "I think you should repaint the van."

"There's nothing wrong with that paint job," Wild Karl growled. "As a professional, I know when a vehicle needs painting and when it doesn't."

Hilda crossed her arms, the way she always did when she was lost for words. She opened her mouth, then closed it without saying anything. It was obvious no one really knew what we should do.

"Listen, everybody," I said. "A whole bunch of people are looking for us. Most of them know exactly what the van looks like. The best thing we could do is disguise it."

Hellie gave me a thumbs up, chewing on her thumbnail to conceal the gesture from the others.

"Have you got any paint here?" Hilda asked Kate.

"If you have, we've got painters, innit," Golden Pete said. He had sat alone and silent on the veranda while Wild Karl was napping. The Summer Shindig had upset him badly as well.

"There might still be some of Jakob's old car paint somewhere," Kate said. "He was always working on some old pile of junk."

Kate's husband Jakob had died ten years ago. She had

decided to continue living in the cottage on her own. We had talked about him on our earlier visit, when she and I sat and chatted on the veranda together. "Alone? I'm not alone!" she had said to lighten the mood. "I've got all my characters with me." That night seemed a very long time ago now.

"Oh, all right," Wild Karl said with a tired wave of his hand. "Gather up whatever's left and paint the van with that. I'm going back to bed."

Kate watched as he walked off. She shook her head, clearly worried about her brother.

While Wild Karl slept, Hellie, Charlie, Golden Pete and I got to work. We had to hold the broken garage door open while we carried things out, otherwise it would have smacked us on the head. The garage was full of stuff. There were old sofas, tools, skis, gardening equipment… As it had been used for storage for the last ten years, every surface was covered.

We spotted the paint cans on a shelf along the rear wall but had to clear everything else out of the way to reach them. There were around twenty cans of paint. We had to prise off the lids with a screwdriver. Some were empty or dried up, but when we mixed together the contents of all the cans, we ended up with a full can of paint. Kate found us some paintbrushes in the cottage. We fixed long handles to a couple of brushes so we could reach the roof of the van.

Then we started painting. From time to time Golden Pete hoisted Hellie on to his shoulders so she could use a long-handled brush to reach the awkward spots that I wouldn't have been brave enough to attempt. Luckily there was just enough paint to cover the whole van.

With our task complete, we went for a swim. Kate promised to dish up huge, bandit-sized portions of ice cream for us when we got back, with chunks of chocolate bars to add on top.

We were just finishing our enormous bowls of ice cream when Wild Karl came downstairs from his second nap.

"What are you lot doing here?" he asked. "Why aren't you painting the van?"

"We've finished," Charlie said. "But—"

"Let him see for himself," Hellie interrupted. "Job done, Boss," she announced in an official tone. "Right out there."

Wild Karl left the kitchen and walked outside. A moment later he dashed back in. His braids looked untidy and he was gasping for breath. "The van," he choked. "Who? How?" He sat down and stared at us without another word.

"What about the van?" Kate asked, trying to get him back on track.

"It's … pink," Wild Karl said. "Totally, utterly pink."

The van was definitely pink. Bright pink. The kind of pink you can't miss. In our defence, we hadn't planned to paint it pink. That was the colour we ended up with when we mixed together all the leftover cans of paint. The good thing was that the van was really hard to recognize now. We couldn't have wished for a better disguise.

CHAPTER 16
in which a serious discussion takes place

We all went outside to look at the van. Wild Karl walked around it. He touched its side and ran his hand along the front grille.

"A pink van," he groaned. "Never, ever in my life did I imagine that I'd be in charge of a pink bandit van."

"You don't have to be," Hilda snapped. "Let Hellie be in charge. It'll be a dream come true for her."

"I didn't mean that," Wild Karl growled.

"Well, I *did* mean it," Hilda replied. "Maybe it's time for you to retire."

I saw Hellie's ears prick up. She was pretending to whittle a stick with her old knife, but her whole body was tense. Was she about to be allowed to lead her own crew? She would be the youngest chief in the bandit world! Not that we could tell anyone. If the other bandits found out, they would just attack the Robbersons and take their money.

"You're talking about something that's not relevant. I've got years ahead of me," Wild Karl said. His eyes were burning with the same fire I saw in Hellie's when she was angry.

"Really?" Hilda asked in a whisper.

Hellie's knife slipped and cut her finger. It was the first time I had ever seen her make a mistake, even a little one.

"Dad," Charlie said in a firm voice. "I want to go to school."

Hellie stood up, put her knife in its sheath and sucked the cut on her finger. She walked off and fished the butterfly knife out of her pocket. She stood in an attack position and practised opening and closing the knife with her weaker hand. *Clack-clack-clack. Clack-clack-clack.* In the past I would have just marvelled at her skill. Now, though, I knew Hellie well enough to tell how upset she was.

"I heard we used to have an apartment," Charlie said. "We could go back there. Park the bandit van in a car park. I could go to school. We could at least take a break, then see what we fancy doing next summer. Once things have calmed down."

His expression seemed to be pleading with me to support him. *Tell them how important it is to go to school,* he begged with his eyes. *Tell them how it feels to sit at your own desk and put your own books in your own rucksack and walk to your own home, where there's a meal waiting.* But I couldn't help him. This matter was for their family to decide.

Sure, it would affect me as well. If the Robbersons decided to stop living in their van, I'd have to go home. My adventure would be over.

"Where'd you hear that?" Hilda demanded.

"Somebody told me," Charlie said, squirming.

"Oh, Kate. Is that the sort of thing you've been telling our children?" Wild Karl said. He looked really sad. "I thought you, of all people…" His voice trailed off and his eyes filled with tears. He left his sentence unfinished and walked away.

Kate seemed to have aged several years. "I didn't mean any harm," she said.

"Dad!" Charlie called after Wild Karl. "It was my fault! I was eavesdropping. Kate was talking to Maisie and I listened in."

But Wild Karl didn't come back and a tense, hopeless silence descended.

The Robbersons spent that evening sulking in their own corners. Meanwhile, I helped Kate make a pot of homemade soup. Just the sort of thing a bandit chief would like, served with big rounds of crispbread. Everyone came to the table but hardly anybody ate anything.

"No thanks," Wild Karl said. "I'm not really hungry."

Hilda dished up some soup for herself but let it go cold in her bowl. She just stared into space. Charlie sat as far from Hellie as possible. They must have had some sort of row. Only Hellie seemed to have an appetite, but she stopped slurping her soup when she realized the others were watching her. The awkward atmosphere round the table seemed strangely familiar. Only as I cleared the untouched dishes from the table did I make the connection: that was how I often felt at home.

"We've got to do something," I wailed to Kate as we sat in the garden swing. We couldn't bear the battle of sulks going on indoors, with everyone avoiding each other.

"It's all right," Kate sighed. "It's good that somebody's finally opened their mouth and said what they want. This is actually pretty mild. A different crew would have risen up in revolt. It has happened. One group tied up their captain and dumped him at a petrol station, then phoned the police on him. This is more complicated because it's a family matter."

"Let's come up with a plan," I said. "We can go over the options and propose the best one."

"If one kid wants to go to school and the other wants to be in charge of the bandit van, they can't both get what they want," Kate said. "I think the problem's bigger than that. For a long time now Karlito has been able to live his own dream. But life isn't always like that. Sometimes you have to get back to reality."

"No!" I exclaimed, leaping up from the swing. I bumped my head on the frame, but that didn't stop me. I regained my footing and said, "There must be a way!"

I couldn't believe I had been kidnapped into a world full of fun and freedom, only for it to suddenly come to a halt.

I mulled things over for three whole days. The pink bandit van stood on the front lawn while everyone moped around on their own. I chewed on the end of my pencil and strolled along the shore of the lake, watching ducklings swim, until some ideas began to take shape in my mind.

I sat down with each of the bandits individually and let them speak their mind. I took notes but didn't show them to anyone, even when they tried to peek over my shoulder.

"Driving a bandit van is a question of image," Wild Karl said. "I mean, you wouldn't ride a motorbike in a tutu! Any bandit knows that!"

"Maths lessons," Charlie whispered, his eyes shining brightly. "Compasses and a set square and equations."

"I think Hilda's right," Hellie said. "I'm totally ready. Let's stop messing about and get on with some real robbing. You can help us."

"It would be so nice to sleep in a bed that didn't smell of engine oil," Hilda said. "Just once in a while."

"All I want is for folk to make their peace," Golden Pete said. "Preferably in a way that makes it look like the boss was right. These young 'uns have to wait their turn. You've got to have a system, even among bandits, innit."

How on earth was I going to combine all of these into a single solution?

ANALYSIS OF THE SITUATION
Noted down by Maisie

1. Wild Karl can't be in charge of a pink bandit van.
2. Wild Karl doesn't want Hellie to be in charge of the bandit van because she's too young. Wild Karl is an adult and the real boss.
3. Wild Karl wants to continue living on the road. That's the only real way to live.
4. Golden Pete wants whatever Wild Karl wants, but he doesn't want to make a big thing of it.
5. Hilda wants a change from sleeping in the van now and then, but she doesn't want to deprive Wild Karl of the things that make him happy.
6. Hellie wants to be in charge of the bandit van, no matter what.
7. Charlie wants to have a normal life and go to school.
8. Kate wishes the family could talk about their dreams and wishes so that they could agree on what to do.

That's as far as I got. The next step would be to write down what Maisie wanted, but it was hard to interview myself. I went for three swims before I knew what I wanted. What I wanted most of all was to solve the Robbersons' conflict. And to spend a few more weeks of this summer holiday with them. Then it would be time for me to head home.

CHAPTER 17

in which Maisie demonstrates how to give a bandit van a makeover

It took another three days to cook up a plan. First I had to outline everything to Kate. She was the only one I could talk to. The other Robbersons were suspicious and monitored my every step. Each of them was convinced I was plotting against them if I spent any time talking to another member of the family.

"Was that a sign?" Wild Karl growled as I handed the pepper across the table to Hellie. "A secret signal? Traitor! We've got a traitor in our midst!"

"No, just pepper for my soup," Hellie said calmly.

Charlie giggled, briefly forgetting that he disagreed with Hellie about everything.

Kate thought my plan was complicated. It was. But the Robbersons' logic was never simple, and so this plan couldn't be simple either.

We used Kate's landline phone to book a taxi into town.

"Going by taxi, are you?" Hilda snapped. "Have you got a problem with my driving?"

The problem was that nobody trusted anyone else. The choice of driver was just as dangerous as passing the pepper to someone. Everyone was on edge and baring their teeth at each other. If I wanted my plan to work, I couldn't ask any of them for help.

"Why is Kate going with you?" Wild Karl asked. "It was us who found you, not Kate! We made a robber out of you. Remember that!"

I promised I'd explain everything when we got back.

"You need to learn to be patient, little bro," Kate said.

Wild Karl gave a snort and stomped upstairs to the attic. He still hadn't forgiven Kate for telling me about their past.

Before the taxi arrived, I had to take both of Hellie's knives off her and explain that she was not to rob the taxi under any circumstances.

The Robberson family stubbornly remained indoors as the taxi drove up. The driver politely accepted one of the mouse farts and didn't seem surprised that I had such a large banknote. To him, I was just a girl heading into town with her auntie. When the driver gave me my change in the shopping mall car park, I could cross one item off my long list of worries. At least the money wasn't forged. Or if it was, it was a really good forgery – meaning it was no longer my problem. We went to a bank and opened an account in Kate's name. Then we paid in most of the cash from the cardboard box. Two bundles of banknotes remained in the box, bound with elastic bands. They would last quite a while. Now that the money was in the bank, there wouldn't be any awkward questions if the van got ambushed by other bandits or searched by police.

They treated us very politely at the bank. The lady at the counter made several attempts to offer us leaflets about shares and investment funds, but we declined. After depositing the cash, we requested a login for online banking. Then we went to the electronics store and bought two laptops and a smart phone. My plan required a certain amount of technical equipment.

At this point Kate insisted on going for a milkshake. She asked me to go over the whole plan again, as she found some of the details difficult to grasp.

"Hang on," she said as I tried to skip over the finer points. "I need to understand all of the ins and outs. I'm an expert at weaving plots, but there's something about that voting business I'm not getting. Explain it again."

As I began to explain it for the third time, I glanced at the neighbouring table to make sure no one was listening to our plan. I was very different from the Maisie who had sat in my dad's car at the start of summer, arguing with my sister. And I didn't want to be that girl any longer. I wanted to save the Robbersons. I wanted it more than anything I had ever wanted in my life.

"So is this what they call a … signature crime?" Kate asked. She tipped up her glass to slurp the last of the milkshake. It left chocolate marks in the corners of her mouth. She was acting like a bandit, leaning over the table as she spoke, narrowing her eyes and trying to make her voice low and hoarse. To me, though, she was just Kate, with chocolate round her mouth. "The kind of thing my brother is always going on about."

She pulled herself up straight before continuing. "Well, you're a real pro at thinking up plots! I'll have to give you a call if Johnny von Dragondorf is in need of a fiendish plan!"

"Any time," I said. "Writing books sounds like fun. And kind of easy!"

Kate half smiled and shook her head. *If you only knew*, she seemed to be saying. "I'm starting to get the impression that robbing is more fun than writing," she said, using her bandit voice again. "WAY more fun than sitting at home. Imagine how shocked Karlito would be if I said I wanted to go along!"

I felt slightly awkward. It had never occurred to me that Kate might actually find our unconventional lifestyle interesting.

Fortunately she dropped the subject of becoming a bandit. "The main thing is that they stop their arguing," she said.

We each ordered another milkshake to go and then headed out to take care of all the other things we needed to do. It was an extensive list, and it took a long time.

"Where on earth have you two been?" Hellie demanded, red-faced, as we drew up to the house in a taxi. "Wild Karl was convinced you'd been arrested. We tried to draw up a diagram of the police station because we thought we'd have to rescue you."

I laughed. "The police have no reason to arrest us," I said. "We've just been out doing some totally legal things."

"For totally bandit-like reasons," Kate added. We both cackled. Then suddenly Kate chucked me on to the grass and I had to struggle for all I was worth to escape from her headlock. Kate Robberson was a woman of steel.

A few days later, five envelopes were delivered to Kate's cottage: three big, thick ones and two smaller ones.

"EriPrint Limited," Charlie sounded out the words on the envelopes. "Maisie, what have you done now?"

As I opened the large envelopes, I called everyone outside to have a look.

"This is the solution to your pink van problem," I told

them. The Robbersons passed the contents of the three large envelopes around, baffled.

"What're we meant to be lookin' at here?" Golden Pete asked. "If I knew somethin' about it, I might be interested, innit."

"You can take your pick," I said, pointing at the stacks of items from the envelopes. "Skulls. Storm clouds and meteors. Ghosts and monsters."

"They're some sort of pictures," Hilda said, cautiously.

"They're car decals," Kate said proudly. I had taught her the technical term when we were having our milkshakes. She had repeated it in the taxi so many times that I'd had to ask her to stop. "People can use them to decorate their vehicles however they like."

"Skulls," Wild Karl said confidently. He was starting to look like the bandit chief I'd first encountered again.

"Ghosts and monsters," Charlie said. "Oh please, I want ghosts!"

"No, definitely skulls," Wild Karl insisted. "As long as I'm in charge of this van, we're having skulls. They're classic. Stylish. They inspire fear and respect. But where on earth did you steal them from?" he asked, furrowing his brows.

Ignoring his question, I unfolded the skull stickers. They were so big that two or three would be enough to cover the whole side of the van. "The best thing is that they're completely removable," I said.

Everyone in the garden was silent.

"Picture this." I grinned. "You put the skulls on the van and do a kiosk heist. Then you escape into a side road, stop and peel off the stickers. You can continue merrily on your way. If you disguise yourselves, you won't have to hide. As long as you remember to cover up your number plates so nobody can trace them, everybody will be looking for the wrong van."

"Wow," Hellie said.

Her amazement was the best compliment she could have given me.

"And then you've got these," I said, waving the two smaller packets. "Two emergency kits for REALLY tricky situations. One is a set of stickers with the name of a florist's shop. The other is a band logo with a bunch of autographs to make the van look like a tour bus. You could park right in front of a police station and not get arrested."

"A signature crime," Wild Karl gasped. "We're going to be the most feared bandit clan in the whole of Finland."

You may be the only free bandit clan, I thought. That was the main reason I had come up with the plan. I could practically sense the fury of the imprisoned bandit gangs. They would do anything to capture the Robbersons. And I would do anything to make sure that didn't happen.

"Is it OK if I show Hellie how to get hold of more

of these?" I asked.

The adults agreed. They started unfolding the skull decals and smoothing them out, ready to stick on to the van. Golden Pete and Wild Karl joked around, the way they used to. Wild Karl gave Kate a playful poke in the ribs as they stuck on the first decal. They seemed to have put their conflict behind them. Even so, lots of things still needed to be sorted out.

CHAPTER 18
in which robbing enters the 21st century

Hellie and I were sitting in the garden swing. I had the laptop on my lap. I had just been showing her how to order more decals for the van and pay for them with Kate's bank details.

"All right," she said, cracking her knuckles. "Let's hear the rest."

"You what?" I asked in amazement. I had thought she'd be overloaded with information.

"That tiny little routine can't be the only thing you can do on here," she said. "How do you track somebody? How can you do a hold-up and say, 'Your sweeties or your life'?"

She tapped on the laptop screen and added, "If there are shops in here, then there must also be kiosks you can rob, right?"

"Oh," I said, completely stumped. "That hadn't even

crossed my mind."

"Well, put it into your mind now," Hellie barked. "Where there are people, there's plenty of stuff. And where there's plenty of stuff, that's a good place for a bandit. Think!"

I thought about my dad sitting at his computer late into the night. He liked to play a quiz that was the most boring game I could think of, but he was unbeatable. Or he'd sit and wait for an online auction to end. He collected old coins – the older the better. He kept them in a glass display case in his office at home. They were a treasure that was worthless to the Robbersons.

When he got wrapped up in an online auction, my dad transformed into a different person. "Stupid automatic bidder! I'll beat you yet," he'd say.

If he did win an auction, a few days later a new coin would arrive in a cardboard box or Jiffy bag. He'd take the coin out and cradle it like a tiny baby. He'd study it under a magnifying glass, totally transfixed.

"My golden beauty," he'd say. "Over here you go, into Jon's treasure chest. There. Now you've got lots and lots of friends." With that, he'd put the coin into the velvet-lined case and lock the lid.

I can't remember him ever speaking so tenderly to Primrose and me.

"I think online heists are different," I told Hellie. "You can't just frighten people into handing over their things.

You have to trick them into really wanting something stupid."

Hellie sat and stared at the screen. Her mind was whirring away. I got up from the swing and went to help Kate prepare dinner. I thought that would be the end of online theft.

I should have known better.

That evening we sat in the sauna for a long time. Finally the Robbersons were able to relax together. Afterwards, we all sat in the kitchen, pink-cheeked, enjoying the warmth of the stove and eating pancakes. Golden Pete was still telling stories about old heists, which he'd started in the sauna.

"Remember when we were on the run from the cops in Kummola," he said, breaking into a cackle. "Who would've thought a hefty copper could run so fast? He was afraid he'd never be allowed to set foot in his home again, innit."

"We'd nicked some tights and a pair of high heels for Hilda," Hellie explained. "From his wife's car."

Hilda smirked.

"She needed them for the midsummer dance," Wild Karl said. "It didn't say on the car that it belonged to the local police chief's wife." He recalled another heist. "What about that amateur detective who followed the tyre tracks to our camp. Where was that one?"

"Somewhere round Hanko way, little place on the coast," Golden Pete said. "I remember I had a stomach bug and the roads were all twisty and turny, innit."

"He actually reached the tent," Charlie said. "I was just little then and really scared."

"The guy looked like a broken folding chair," Wild Karl said.

"A total Salary Sam," Hellie said. She puckered her lips to imitate the man's speech: "Wiw you pwease give me my umbwewwa back. The tweats and fizzy dwinks you can keep but let me have my umbwewwa. It's been in my famiwy for genewations."

They all laughed. Hellie was talented at everything, but she was absolutely brilliant at impressions.

"Dad sent him flying," Charlie said proudly. "And chucked the umbrella after him. We didn't need it. We had used it as a temporary tent pole, but then we found the actual one inside a sleeping bag."

"He can be strong when he wants to, our old grizzly bear," Hilda said. She stretched out her toes.

"That's it," Kate said as she leaped up. "I want to come with you! I'm sick and tired of listening to your stories. I'm coming along in the bandit van. You just try to chuck me out. I beat Karlito at wrestling every time. I'm not some old granny or silly writer who you need to come and visit out of pity once or twice a year. I want to live dangerously too!"

At that point, the argument kicked off again.

"Absolutely not," Wild Karl said. He also got up from the table. "This is getting out of hand. I've got kids wanting to take over the van, a wife who's starting a mutiny, and now a sister who wants to tag along after going on for ten years about how irresponsible I am to live a life others only dream about."

"Don't exaggerate," Hilda said. "I said it would be nice to sleep in clean sheets. That's hardly a mutiny."

"Everybody, listen," I said. "I have a suggestion."

"Well," Wild Karl said, holding out his hands. "Out with it. Do you want to be in charge of the van as well?"

"Not exactly," I said. "I want to take you all on a trip tomorrow."

"Yay!" Charlie exclaimed. "Let's take packed lunches!"

"There are three conditions," I said.

"This girl's learned how to haggle," Golden Pete said. "She'll make an unbeatable boss someday. Better hold on to your seat, Karl."

Wild Karl slapped his forehead in despair. "Things can't get any worse. Now we've got children dictating terms," he said. "All right, let's hear them."

"Number one," I said, raising my index finger. "No one is allowed to argue or criticize the plan until you've heard every aspect of it."

"Fine," Hellie said.

"Very well," Wild Karl said, glancing to see if the others objected. "All right with us."

"Two," I said, holding up another finger. "We're taking the bandit van, and Kate gets to drive."

"Have you got a driving licence, Kate?" Hellie asked, sounding shocked.

"Well, then, I'm not going," Hilda said, crossing her arms.

"But we need you to come along," I urged.

"Go on," Wild Karl said. He went over to Hilda and put his arms round her. "There's no such thing as a nice trip if you're not there with us. You keep our spirits up. You make sure your old man doesn't get into rows with everybody."

"All right," Hilda said, blushing slightly. "But just this time."

"Yes!" Charlie and Kate said in unison. They high-fived each other.

"Wicked, Maisie," Hellie said with a grin like the Cheshire Cat. "Well played."

"What?" Wild Karl said, snapping his head round to look at Hellie.

"Nothing, Boss," Hellie said. "I just know where this is all heading."

"What's the third condition?" Golden Pete asked impatiently. "Will we get to rob some folks? If that's on the cards, then you can count me in! It's been totally boring these last few days, innit."

"Yes, what's the third condition?" Kate asked, turning to me. She knew very well what it was.

"The third condition is that if the plan works out and you're happy with it, you will take me back home." Then I added, "To be more precise: you will return me to the car park outside our apartment, in the same condition I was in when you stole me."

An almighty racket began. I left the kitchen and went to wait on the veranda while they sorted themselves out.

A moment later, Kate joined me and said, "They agree." Then she added, "This is a huge risk, Maisie. Are you sure we're doing the right thing?"

We had gone over the plan three times at the café and made some more tweaks. It was really our joint plan. That didn't make the knot in my stomach feel any smaller though.

"We'll just have to find out," I said.

CHAPTER 19

in which they go on a trip and Maisie's plan becomes clear

The pink bandit van, now decorated with skulls, drove off from Kate's cottage at ten in the morning. Up until then every member of the Robberson clan had been fishing for information about where we were heading.

"Out with it," Hellie said bluntly. She invited me to practise knife-throwing with her, which I knew was an excuse to press me for details. "You know you want to tell me."

"No, I don't," I said. I grinned and threw my knife at the target, which was fixed to a birch tree. I got eight points without really aiming – I guess I was getting better at it.

"Yeah, right," Hellie laughed. "I didn't really want to know. I was just asking."

"You were just testing me to see if anything slipped out," I said.

She nodded and we high-fived. At the start of this summer I never would have believed we'd become such good friends.

"Will I get to go to school?" Charlie asked. "Is that included in your plan? Or did you forget about me?" He kept asking as we carried the sleeping bags out to the van. I had told everyone we were going on an overnight trip.

"I know we haven't really talked since the argument, but we used to discuss it a lot. It's harder to talk properly now that we don't sleep next to each other," he said. "I'm worried that you've only considered people's wishes that have to do with robbing. I mean, that's fine. Bandit clans *should* think about that stuff. Don't laugh, but I've been wondering if you've started to think that robbing is the only thing that matters, not the ordinary things that I want. After all, you get to go to school this autumn no matter what."

We rolled up our sleeping bags carefully. The van was jam-packed because we had an extra person in addition to our usual stuff. A second extra person, I should say. I wasn't officially part of the van's crew, though I wished I was.

"By the way, I knew you didn't want to be here in the autumn," Charlie said. "We've never talked about it, but I just knew."

"Take it easy in first gear, gun it in second," Hilda said. She had squeezed into the front of the van between Wild Karl and Kate, who was in the driver's seat. Hilda was trying to pretend it wasn't crowded and uncomfortable. There was plenty of room in the row behind, but Hilda would never agree to sit in the back.

"Spin the wheels! Make them spin!" Hilda ordered as Kate started creeping off in first gear.

"I am NOT tearing up the grass on my own front lawn," Kate snapped.

Hilda was quiet. I could see Wild Karl's belly tremble with silent laughter.

Kate and I had refused to reveal our destination. At first, they tried to guess where we were going every time we came to a junction. But one by one the Robbersons drifted off and after four hours on the road they were all in a deep sleep. The name of the city we were headed to started to appear on road signs, but everyone was asleep.

"Are you sure this is a good idea?" I asked Kate. She skilfully steered the van towards the city centre.

"I should've done this years ago," she replied.

"Wakey wakey," I said in a gentle voice when we had reached our destination. Kate switched off the engine and, according to plan, started to hand out cups of hot chocolate to the sleepy passengers. "Now listen, everyone," I continued. "We're here to check out a possible place to stay. We'll take the sleeping bags and packed lunches and head up there –

174

for one night. Then you'll get to hear the rest of the plan."

Hilda suddenly noticed something and set her cup down on the dashboard. "Karl," she said. "We're home."

Wild Karl and Hilda undid their seat belts, got out and stood in the car park, holding their steaming cups of hot chocolate. We'd driven all day. It was almost six o'clock and now August was approaching, the days were getting shorter. You could tell that it was nearly evening.

"The Christmas star is gone from the window," Hilda said.

"We're not going up to the fifth floor," I said. "For one thing, it wasn't available."

"I'm sorry," Kate said. "It was the first place we checked."

"It would be too small for you, with just two bedrooms," I said. "We're going to the sixth floor instead."

"What's the meaning of this?" Wild Karl snarled. "What exactly are you playing at, Kate?"

"Let's go inside," I said.

Everyone finished their hot chocolate and took as much as they could carry: sleeping bags, baskets, cool boxes. The lift was full, so Charlie and I decided to take the stairs up to the sixth floor. Charlie looked shocked when I took a key out of my pocket and opened the door to Apartment B20.

As I called everyone into the living room, I looked out of the window to the car park below, where the bandit van was cooling off in its parking space.

"Who lives here?" Wild Karl asked me. "Don't say you've stolen someone's flat. Even we're never that cruel."

"I live here," Kate said. "I bought this apartment for myself, under my own name, two days ago. I'm going to live here, whether you like it or not. I've been thinking for a long time it would be nice to come back to the city."

"What about the cottage?" Wild Karl exclaimed.

"What about it? A person is allowed to have a summer cottage, aren't they?" Kate said. "But listen. Now you get to hear Maisie's plan."

It took some time for everyone to unroll their sleeping bags on the floor and sit down on them. I remained standing, leaning against the radiator as I tried to summon up some courage. I took out my diary, even though I knew every detail by heart.

"I'll remind you once again that you promised to listen to my entire proposal before you say what you think of it," I said. "I'll go over what each of you wished for."

I began reading from my notes.

- Wild Karl can't be in charge of a pink bandit van.

"This bit of the situation has changed," I added. "The van is no longer pink – it can be decorated with

176

whatever design you want. You can buy car paint from the same company that makes the decals if you want to change its colour entirely."

- Wild Karl wants to continue as boss and make the Robbersons into the most feared bandit clan in Finland.
- Hilda wants to sleep in a proper bed occasionally.

"But also be a bandit on the road," I added.

- Hellie wants to be in charge of her own van.
- Golden Pete wants things to be the way they used to be.
- Charlie wants to go to school.
- Kate wants to become a bandit. She doesn't want to live in the cottage on her own any longer. She wants to see her relatives more often.

At this point Wild Karl was about to voice an objection, but Hilda and Kate tackled him to the floor and put a hand over his mouth.

"Here's my proposal," I said. My mouth went dry. "In the future, you will have two home bases. One is the bandit van, same as before. The other is this apartment. It's got four bedrooms. One for Hilda and Wild Karl. One for Golden Pete. Hellie and Charlie each get their own room. Kate says she'd prefer to sleep in the living room, as it's easier when she's writing. The apartment is in Kate's name, so nobody will ask any questions."

"What about our robbing, if we're just hanging out here?" Hellie blurted out. Instantly realizing she'd broken her promise, she added, "Sorry."

"Robbing will be done in two shifts," I said. "Weekdays will be Hilda, Wild Karl, Golden Pete and Hellie, whenever she wants. Hilda will be the driver, with Wild Karl in command."

Everyone remained quiet. They glanced at one another. Charlie looked at the floor. I could see how tense he was. He curled his hands into fists.

"On the weekend shift will be Kate, Hellie and Charlie, plus Golden Pete, whenever he wants," I said. "Kate will be the driver, with Hellie in command."

"Now just a— Oops," Wild Karl said, quickly holding up his hands before anyone shushed him. "I'm listening! I'm listening!"

"Anyone not on a robbing shift will spend their off-duty time here," I said. "Relaxing, sleeping in a proper bed, making plans for heists that will bring new meaning to robbing."

I looked at Hellie and Wild Karl as I said that bit.

I continued, "And in addition, anyone who wants to can go to school. No arguments. Everyone can use their free time however they like, as long as they don't endanger anyone else. Now some additional conditions to make sure this plan works. One: No robbing in the local area. The robbing zone begins one hundred kilometres from home base. If anyone notices the van, you must change the decals. If there's any trouble, drive to the cottage or another safe place mentioned in the atlas and drive a different vehicle back to home base."

Hellie nodded and looked out of the window. It was hard to tell whether she approved of the plan or thought it was terrible.

"Two: The shift teams will not compete with each other or become enemies. The reason for having two teams is to expand the Robbersons' reputation and to make robbing fun. Robbing is not necessary during the off season, but anyone who wants to go robbing can do so to their heart's content."

Hilda was looking at me, and I could tell she was getting emotional. She didn't dare to glance over at Wild Karl.

"Three: This plan may change at any time, provided you all agree on the details and the change is fair to everyone. Kate will be in charge of monitoring this part of the agreement."

"Can I ask a question?" Hellie piped up. "What about you? Are you trying to say you're just going to forget about us and go back to your stupid school?"

I smiled and recited the final bit. "If the weekend captain

agrees, that team may add one additional member when a heist is planned for southern Finland."

"There you have it – that's the plan," Kate said, clapping her hands together. "Now it's time to vote."

We had reached the point that I had thought over constantly, but couldn't predict. I had imagined all different situations – where they might be happy, angry or disapproving. Now that the moment was here, I understood that it was impossible to prepare myself for it. Everything depended on this.

CHAPTER 20

in which there is a vote that determines
Maisie and the Robbersons' future

Kate explained how the voting would work. I sank down against the radiator – all my energy was gone.

"There are a total of six votes," Kate said. "Karl, Hilda, Hellie, Charlie, me and Golden Pete. There has to be a majority: at least four votes either way."

"Why do you get to vote?" Wild Karl asked. "Of course you're in favour of the plan. You get to vote to go out robbing, no discussion. So that's how it is, eh? You just come along and sign up?"

I was starting to worry that Wild Karl's hurt feelings were preventing him from seeing the good aspects of the plan. He could only see how many things were going to change.

"I hope I'm as much a part of this family as Golden Pete," Kate said tactfully. "And if Charlie wants to go to school while you're out robbing, it might be good to have an adult around."

"Come on, let's vote," Charlie said. "I say yes!"

"Me too!" Hellie exclaimed. "We should all say yes at the same time!"

"I was thinking we ought to mark our choices on slips of paper," Kate said. "But we could just raise our hands."

"I'm voting the same way the boss votes, innit," Golden Pete said.

"No, you have to vote for yourself," Hilda snapped. "Preferably before he votes, so you're not just tagging along behind him."

"I'm voting in favour of the plan," Kate said calmly. "It has a lot of advantages, not just for me. You won't have to stay in my freezing cottage in the winter – you won't have to pay the price for robbing."

"We've been really lucky," Hilda said, "that nobody has been seriously ill."

"I'm against it," Wild Karl growled. "You better believe I'm against it. What are you lot playing at? You think you can take power away from me? The young ones are plotting a takeover and everybody says, 'Good idea!'? In the old days people would at least hijack a vehicle for themselves and start their own gang. Now you're driving a wedge into your own group. You're forcing me to retire in the midst of everything!"

"No, it's a holiday," Hilda said. "Even you need a holiday once in a while."

"If you think that way, Boss, then I'm against it too," Golden Pete said. "I know you're only thinkin' of what's best for us all."

I sensed that the plan was about to collapse. I doodled some flowers in my diary. Hellie, Charlie and Kate were in favour, Wild Karl and Golden Pete were against. Hilda hadn't said what her view was. The outcome looked frighteningly clear: nothing would change. They would carry on driving around in the bandit van the same as before, and the people in the back seat would have no say.

"Don't you get it?" Wild Karl said. "If I vote yes, Maisie will go home. She's made us forget that last condition. Clever move, but I can see through her attempts to distract us. Maisie helps us to think better. At long last we were able to go out robbing this summer without Hellie and Charlie whingeing and moaning in the back seat the whole time. We would have triumphed in every event at the Summer Shindig. We've got a new signature crime – three, in fact. We are feared and respected more than ever. There is no way I'd vote yes and let Maisie leave."

"Didn't you just say the young ones were trying to mutiny?" Kate said. "What do you think about Maisie being the one who initiated this mutiny?"

"And if Maisie helps us to think, why aren't you

thinking?" Hellie said. "Why can't you see the good bits of the plan?"

"If you're voting specifically on whether to make Maisie stay," Hilda reasoned, "then I'm voting yes. It's time she went back home. The place for every child is in their own home – at least when they want to go home. No pig-headed bandit chief should prevent her from leaving."

Silence fell over the room. Wild Karl opened and closed his fists, as if he felt his power slipping away through his hands.

"We win!" Hellie exclaimed, dancing with joy. "We win! We win!"

"Hang on," Wild Karl snapped. "I'm not having this. As the head of this bandit clan, I'm not having it. This has all gone too fast. You all gave your views too fast. We've never decided anything by voting before. Things were decided when they were decided."

"Yes, Dad, you made all the decisions," Charlie said, with a new edge in his voice.

"We had an agreement, Karlito. You said you wouldn't go back on your word," Kate said. "Unless you want to lose your standing in the eyes of the younger generation."

"That's not what I meant," Wild Karl said. "This business about letting the majority decide is what bothers me. We bandits have always done things unanimously. That's how it should be. I'm changing my mind, and I am fully entitled to do so. It's my right as the chief, the head of the family and … and … the oldest male person. I don't want to disagree with Hilda. I don't want anybody to think about this vote later on and think they were on the losing side. It's best if we're unanimous, so there won't be any grumbling."

"Yes, of course you can change your mind," Kate said, glancing sideways at me. "Does anyone else want to change their mind?"

Golden Pete raised his hand. "Clearly new information has come to light, innit. So yep."

"Maisie's proposal has been approved unanimously," Kate said. She rapped her knuckles against the radiator.

I would get to go home, which meant my summer in the bandit van would soon be over.

CHAPTER 21

in which the bandits' reputation gets around, for better or for worse

This is such a pain, I thought to myself as I taped up copies of the new rules on all the doors and in the hallway. Hellie followed me around. She just watched as my hair got stuck to the tape and sheets of paper escaped, floating to the floor. We were alone together in the apartment. The others had gone out robbing – they said they wanted to get a couple of rugs and a quilt.

The Robbersons still had no concept about the value of money or how much wealth they had, and I wasn't going to explain it to them. If their minds were set on stealing a quilt and they wanted to ambush ten cars to do it, that was up to them.

The tape started sticking to itself in my hands. I lost my cool.

"You're just trying to get this done so you can get out of here," Hellie said.

"I don't want to get out of here," I said.

"Sure," Hellie said. "That's why it's better if you believe we won't cope without you."

She was so frighteningly right that I burst out laughing.

She started choreographing self-defence moves with her butterfly knife, in total violation of Rule 9.

"Well, will you cope?" I spluttered.

"Are you serious?" she replied, attempting to work in a series of kung-fu-style high kicks. I admired the way she landed silently after every leap, as if she had pads in her feet. "I reckon Golden Pete will mess things up within a couple of months. He's so excited now that he gets to be an urban pirate. I can't see the others doing that well either."

It seemed to me that even two weeks would be an optimistic estimate.

NEW RULES - IMPORTANT!
Noted down by Maisie

The Robbersons now have two main bases: the bandit van and this apartment. To keep the apartment safe from the police, the following new set of rules must be obeyed.
1. No robbing within a 100-kilometre radius of the apartment.
2. That 100-kilometre rule also includes minor acts of

nicking, "borrowing" and finding.

3. No following the neighbours "just to check which flat they live in".

4. No pestering the building caretaker for the spare keys to other apartments.

5. Charlie's schoolmates and Kate's friends and anyone else's friends are also part of the no-robbing zone, even if they live outside it.

6. Do not mention robbing to anyone outside your own bandit crew.

7. Do not brag about robbing or tell stories or jokes about robbing.

8. Do not make threats like, "Nice jacket you've got there. It'd be a shame if a bandit van just happened to come along…"

9. The use of eye patches, pirate flags, knives or other weapons within the no-robbing zone is strictly prohibited.

10. Singing tunes in the shower about robbing or pirates, such as "Robin Hood," "Yo Ho Ho" or any made-up songs, is prohibited because the sound travels through the pipes to other apartments.

At last I had taped up every copy of the rules.

"Forget it," Hellie said as she threw her knife over her shoulder with such force, its handle vibrated when it landed in the door frame. "Maybe we shouldn't live in a permanent place like other people. We're used to being on the move. Charlie needs to accept that that's how things are when you're a bandit. When's the last time you practised throwing at a target, anyway?" she said, concerned. "You'll lose your skill if you don't train regularly."

She placed the knife Kate had given me into my hand. How on earth could she have known where I kept it?

Then she raised my hand into throwing position. "You need to work on your floppy left wrist. It always pulls too far to the left," she said.

So I started practising knife-throwing against the newly painted wall in the front hall. It was clear the Robbersons would never be ordinary flat-dwellers.

Hellie observed my throwing for half an hour. She corrected my finger position and posture. She was a surprisingly good teacher. She sat on the hall floor with her knees pulled up to her chest. Whenever I threw less than a seven, she issued a new instruction.

"You're feeling down," she said at the end. "That's why your throwing is so inconsistent. Hey, let me show you something."

She went into the living room and opened the laptop. I had shown her how to use the internet a few weeks earlier. Now she was typing in passwords and search terms in the blink of an eye.

"I boosted its performance with a couple of my own

tricks," she said calmly. "Check these out. There's nothing for you to worry about."

She showed me her page on an auction site. It said: *Twenty auctions in progress.*

"I've launched a bandit operation that's going so well, we'll soon be able to buy up a few more apartments around Finland if we want," she said. "You said you needed to convince people they really, really want some really stupid thing. Here's an example."

I looked at the listing for item 41325545. It was a customized anarchist-style Barbie doll with a "Bandit H" trademark logo. The doll sported a red Mohican hairstyle, a piercing in the back of its neck and a black leather miniskirt made from the jacket we'd stolen from a car on the west coast.

"One hundred and forty-nine euros!" I exclaimed.

"The record is 620, paid by some collector in Germany," Hellie said. There was no emotion in her voice.

"But ... how?"

"You can't see it here, but if you go into a password-protected part of the Bandit H site there's a notice saying the items are customized with only stolen and found objects," she said. "And then there's a discussion forum for anarchist lifestyles and stuff. Couple of thousand visitors a day."

She went to another site. I scanned down the messages.

"That purple section is locked. You get login details to access it when you buy a doll. That's what they're really after, for some reason," she explained, shaking her head. "Here, I'll show you something else." Her fingers flew across the keyboard. "Guess who this is," she said, pointing to a user profile. *Beach Barbie, 22*, it said. "That's AK Mikkonen of the Offshore Raiders. She really wants to work for me. I haven't decided yet whether I should let her."

"Well, at least she hasn't been caught," I said. "The robbing continues, just with new methods."

"I thought it would be good if you knew about this," Hellie said as she hid the page again.

"Money," I said.

"Mouse farts have never interested me," she snapped. "Kate manages the bank accounts and postage and business stuff on her laptop. I'm underage. I'm only interested in robbing and human nature."

Hellie went to the fridge, took out the milk and put twenty spoonfuls of cocoa powder into it. Then she put the lid on, shook it and started drinking the chocolate milk straight from the bottle.

"But what am I supposed to do about all these requests for interviews?" she asked. "*Elle* magazine wants to do a feature on young designers. They bought one of the dolls I designed last month. Then the rumour mills started up and other magazines have joined the queue."

Just then, the door opened and the noisy bandit crew came in.

"We got the rug we were after," Charlie called out. "The boss was about to give up, but I said to check in the boot and there it was, rolled up. So Guess & Grab was useful after all."

"Shut the door," Hellie ordered. "Shut the door before you shout about anything. Amateurs!"

CHAPTER 22

which features a shopping trip - Robberson-style

Our trip to the supermarket was a complete disaster. It had started with good intentions. I was beginning to worry about the effort the Robbersons put into acquiring things for their bandit headquarters, down to every towel and box of eggs. They still needed a lot of furnishings for the apartment, which meant there was nearly always someone in the van scouting for items. I thought I'd show the bandit clan a more convenient way to get food at least. In hindsight, I should have known better.

At the cottage, Auntie Kate shopped for everything they wanted and filled up the fridge. She had a six-month supply of mustard and heavy-duty crispbread on hand. All the basics to tide them over while they waited for the next car loaded with sweets to come along. But the school year would be starting soon and fewer cars carrying packed lunches were out on the country roads. Most cars were travelling in the opposite direction now, everybody returning home with boxes of blackcurrants and bags of apples. The summer's harvest was on its way to freezers in the city. It wasn't the right sort of food for a bandit chief. Wild Karl needed sausages and eggs and meatballs and pasties to pile on his crispbread. He'd never agree to live on stolen packets of instant soup for more than a day or two.

I told Kate what I planned to do. I wanted to run my idea past her first, in case it was so bad I should just forget about it.

"Are you sure it'll work?" she asked. "I've started to wonder if there's some deeper reason my brother doesn't deal with money. I don't mind going shopping. I think it's nice to have a family to shop for."

"Maybe it is a bad idea," I said. "I just thought it would be good to show them how it works."

"So things will go smoothly here when you're back at home. I see," Kate said slowly. "The day may come when I'm ill or can't carry all the milk Golden Pete manages to get through. All right. Let's go, then once you're at home, I'll sit down with Hellie and make sure she understands everything. That'll work. Don't you worry."

My instincts told me things might go spectacularly wrong, so I didn't take the Robbersons to the nearest corner shop. Instead, we drove to a huge superstore fifteen kilometres away.

"Nice to have everybody back in the van again," Hilda said as she followed the signs to the car park. "The load feels right."

"You don't slide around on the seats when there's no free space," Charlie said. "I've missed Maisie's carsick face!"

"I don't get car sick," I said and was about to start wrestling with him when I remembered I needed to give instructions.

"This is not a heist," I told them for the fourth time, and again for the fifth. I was standing in front of them in the boiling-hot car park, like a sergeant addressing troops. "This is not a signature crime. It is not anything even resembling a crime. We are on a training mission."

"Right. Training," Wild Karl said knowingly. "It makes sense to do that once in a while. Didn't I say that, Pete, when we met up with Sandvik to compare techniques before the Summer Shindig five years ago? Kind of like sizing each other up. In this job it's all about learning by doing. Then Sandvik got arrested at the end of that summer, so I guess he didn't learn while he was doing."

"Hellie, put your knife away," I said. "Now everybody repeat after me: This is not a heist."

They all said it in unison – except Golden Pete, who dragged out the "… not a heist" at the end.

"Can we go in now?" Hilda asked. She watched in amazement as other families inched into the nearby parking spaces, got out of their vehicles in an orderly fashion and headed towards the main entrance. In her competitive world view, we'd got off to a strong start but were now being left behind.

"First, let's put on our disguises," I said as I handed out various items. I had a beach bag filled with a variety of things left over from recent heists: sunglasses, scarves, baseball caps. I gave Hellie a bright pink cap, which she glared at with disgust. "And these," I added, handing her a pair of gaudy 1960s-style sunglasses.

"No way am I wearing this," Wild Karl said, holding a Hawaiian shirt that we had been using as a temporary curtain in the van's rear window.

"I can take that one, Boss," Golden Pete said as a gesture of self-sacrifice.

"There are CCTV cameras inside," I warned. "If – IF – anything goes wrong in there, you do not want any security staff or police to recognize you in the videos."

"Smart girl," Kate said. She leaned against Hellie for support as she stuffed the skirt of her summer dress into a pair of neon-green cycling shorts.

"You don't need to do that!" I exclaimed. "Those shorts

are just in case of an emergency."

"If everybody else is going to look like a clown, then I will too," Kate said decisively.

When we finally headed over to the entrance, I had to try really hard not to laugh at how silly they looked. But so did every family coming from the beach on that hot day. Then again, none of the other dads were dressed in a beach kaftan with a deep neckline and long tassels that trailed behind them like cheerful flags. I tried to reassure myself. Even if we did attract some odd looks, nobody would suspect we were Finland's most-wanted bandit gang.

"All right. This is where you get your shopping trolley," I explained. "You need a trolley so you can put the groceries in it."

"Sounds good," Wild Karl said.

They each took a trolley, even though I said that one or two per family was enough. At first Wild Karl wanted everyone to proceed one after the other in order of importance – with him in front, obviously. On their way to the fruit and veg aisle they looked more like a train than the holidaying family I had tried to disguise them as.

"Not all in a line!" I hissed. "People wander around and browse in a supermarket. Look at how everyone else is just going where they like. Maybe it's better if you each go off and focus on your own thing."

I stopped the trolley caravan and calmly explained how

to find the vegetables and bread, meat, milk, cereal and sweets.

"There are signs hanging up above," I told them. "They show the names of the most common items. Or you can ask a shop assistant. Shall we meet up by the sweets? We'll all be heading there anyway."

"We'll meet by the sweets," Hellie said to show she understood my instructions. After a few strides to build up speed, she lifted her feet off the ground and glided into the crowd of shoppers on her trolley, as if she'd been doing it her whole life.

They gradually disappeared in different directions.

I stayed with Kate to pick up some essentials: packets of hot-dog buns, little round cheeses, the best kind of sausages, streaky bacon, eggs. It was hard to remember what I used to shop for with Mum and Dad. Primrose only wanted health foods, but she'd stand and gaze at the sweets near the tills. I couldn't remember what I used to pester my parents for. I had memories of reluctantly following Dad as he pushed the trolley. So many things were going to change when I got home.

Our trolley was starting to fill up with groceries.

"Shall we go round and see what the others are up to?" Kate suggested. "At least no alarms have gone off yet."

We passed the bakery section and headed towards the meat aisle. I was sure we'd find Golden Pete and Wild

Karl there, piling their trolleys high with sausages and meat for barbecuing. But they weren't there and nor were the others.

"He could be buying absolutely anything," Kate said fearfully. "Karlito's never been in a supermarket before…"

Then we heard a massive crash from the next aisle. A member of staff glanced up but then returned to filling the fridges. We went round the other way and broke into a run. A red-faced Wild Karl stood in the canned goods aisle. Some distance away I saw Golden Pete scampering after an old lady, clearly waiting for the right moment. When she turned to reach for a jar of gherkins, Golden Pete grabbed a packet of ground coffee from her trolley and dashed over to us with it. He said nothing, just held up the coffee in triumph as if he'd broken the marathon world record.

"Bloody difficult, this," Wild Karl said. He was out of breath. "Loads of people around, not much time to act. You need to be in shape."

"Got to know what to go for, innit," Golden Pete said as he placed the packet of coffee in Wild Karl's trolley. "Got to move real quick, like."

They didn't have many items in their trolley.

"You know, Maisie, I'm not at all sure this saves any time versus robbing cars," Wild Karl said.

"But surely you don't think you're meant to steal things from other people's trolleys?" I asked, baffled.

So we started over, this time from the very beginning.

They had all misunderstood various things. Hilda had swapped her trolley for a more interesting one that was filled with somebody else's items for their young family. In addition to ready meals, they had jars of baby food, which Hilda was merrily chucking out of the trolley as I arrived. Meanwhile Hellie had decided to sneak into the back office and got hold of the staff members' keys and a shift rota. Charlie was transfixed by the CCTV cameras and had forgotten all about shopping. I found him staring right up at one camera, following it as it pivoted from one shelf to another. I could only imagine how much video they had of him in close-up.

"This isn't working," I said to Kate.

"Don't say that. There's a first time for everybody," she reassured me.

After two sweaty hours and endless advice, guidance and corrections, the Robbersons had reached the checkout tills. It was a quiet time in the afternoon, so there were no queues.

"Are you sure you need that much?" I asked Hilda. Her trolley was now filled with crispbread and mustard.

"Absolutely," she said, placing her arms across the top of her items to shield them.

Charlie's trolley was piled high with all kinds of biscuits and sweets. Wild Karl had finally found the meats and bacon.

Worried, I glanced at Kate, who nodded encouragingly.

"Even if they decided to buy every single thing in the store, that would be fine," she said. "They've got the money."

I motioned for them to come closer so we could put all the trolleys through the same till. Then Kate could pay for everything with her debit card.

Just then, Wild Karl let out a bandit yell: "Everybody into position!"

All the Robbersons spread out. They looked fierce and determined.

"Run for it!"

At precisely the same moment, all five of them started racing towards the tills and straight past them. Alarms started shrieking. The buckles on Hellie's combat boots jangled as she pushed her trolley at breakneck speed towards the exit and the car park.

"Good heavens," Kate said as we ran after them. "I'm not cut out for running."

Hellie was waiting for everyone by the automatic doors, which opened outwards. Outside, Charlie was rolling a whole column of nested shopping trolleys towards the doors as fast as he could. Hellie and Charlie shoved the trolleys against the doors to prevent them opening. That would slow down the people chasing us. But only a little.

"Run!" Hellie yelled as she dashed past us.

I grabbed Kate's hand and pulled her along behind me.

I waved Charlie on ahead of us.

When Kate and I reached the parking space, the van's engine was already running and all the doors were open. Hellie and Charlie piled the groceries in through the side door while Wild Karl and Golden Pete tipped the contents of two whole shopping trolleys inside. Sausages, chocolate and mustard flew through the air.

The others helped me and Kate inside and the van started to drive off. I saw three security guards and a shop assistant finally manage to climb over the shopping trolley barricade and run towards us, roaring. The car park was in total chaos, with overturned trolleys and round cheeses and fillet steaks and chocolate bars everywhere. Our getaway was anything but clean.

I seized a small handful of banknotes from the grey cardboard box and flung them outside just before Hellie slammed the side door shut.

"Hey! They work," Wild Karl said in amazement. "Now we know how mouse farts work. They cause people to freeze on the spot when you throw them like that."

I looked out of the window. The security guards were busy trying to grab the banknotes as they whirled around the car park in the air currents churned up by the van.

"Thanks for a lovely shopping experience!" I called out.

We cheerfully waved goodbye to the shocked shop assistant who stood and watched us zoom out of sight.

CHAPTER 23

in which they end up in a familiar car park

Three days after our supermarket excursion and the car chase that followed it, I woke the Robberson family with the smell of fried eggs, bacon and meat pasties heated in the oven. (If I'm honest, the pasties got a bit singed while I concentrated on frying the eggs, which is surprisingly difficult.)

Kate got up early too. The deadline for submitting her new Angela Heartwell manuscript was a few days away. She sat in her pink writing robe and watched as I prepared breakfast. Meanwhile, she mouthed lines of passionate dialogue to herself and then tapped them into her laptop. In our first two weeks in the apartment we'd both learned that morning was the best time to get things done in peace. Once the others got up it was total chaos.

"What have we here?" Wild Karl said as he emerged from his bedroom in pyjamas, rubbing his belly. The smell of the singed pasties had worked like an alarm clock. "Are you trying to compete with Hilda's cooking? I could use some food after the strange night I've had. I tried sleeping inside the wardrobe. Now this fine body of mine feels as if it's had all the kinks ironed out of it. I didn't hear any of the snoring Hilda's always complaining about while I was in there. Not even a hint! That's living proof of what I always say: Give a bandit chief a problem and he'll solve it."

Hilda padded into the kitchen after her husband. From the look she gave Kate and me, I guessed she didn't want to discuss the wardrobe experiment.

"You're very welcome to take over kitchen duties," Hilda said to me, stifling a yawn. "Then I can focus on my fast driving."

Golden Pete must have heard our conversation. He scratched his armpits as he came into the hall.

"Did you get any sleep?" I asked him.

"Well," he said, then made a few smacking noises with his mouth. "It's different not having the exhaust pipe rumbling under yer bum when you're sleeping."

Hilda turned towards the bedrooms and called out, "Kids, time to get up. Maisie's made breakfast. You can learn from her and give us grown-ups a nice surprise once in a while."

"Forget it," Charlie said as he shuffled out of his room. "You still won't let us do anything when we're out in the van."

Just then, Hellie came in from outside. She had gone out on a morning recce at the crack of dawn.

I called Kate over to the table. She was in the middle of writing a lovers' quarrel. I had been watching her from the corner of my eye. Every now and then she put her hand on her forehead and seemed ready to faint. At other times she stood up and made sweeping gestures with one hand while the other hand was on her hip. I had never seen an author at work before. It looked both strange and exciting.

"What's the special occasion?" Golden Pete asked as I set plates heaped with food in front of everyone. "Just so I know what we should be congratulating them on, innit."

I plonked two tubes of mustard on the table and wondered where I should begin. I mustn't sound like I was asking or begging. I should just tell them where things stood.

"Don't be silly," Hellie said. "It's obvious. Maisie wants to go back home."

She really was wide awake.

"That reminds me," Charlie piped up. "School starts next Wednesday. I still need to get a couple of books."

Wild Karl was holding a huge piece of crispbread that sagged under all the eggs and sausages he had piled on top.

When he heard what Hellie said and saw my face, he put it back down on his plate. This was the first time I'd ever seen him interrupt his eating. Earlier that summer, no one had been allowed to discuss unpleasant subjects at the table. The memory of the first breakfast I ate outdoors caused a pang of regret inside me. That day in June seemed like years ago now.

"Is Hellie right?" Wild Karl asked. "Wait, that's a foolish question. Hellie's always right. Are you leaving now?"

His voice came out small and almost tearful. I was touched that he seemed to care so much about me. I nodded.

"I thought you were really committed again," Wild Karl said. "Now that you and Hellie have your own room and everything. And the two robbing shifts…"

He choked up and tears began rolling down his cheeks. Hilda got up from the table and went to fetch him a hanky. Wild Karl dabbed his eyes. His tears had completely soaked the hanky to a damp rag. After drying his eyes, he gave his nose a good blow and then handed the hanky back to Hilda, who looked unimpressed as she took it.

"A child's place is at home," Hilda said when she returned from putting her soaked hanky in the laundry basket. "You and I agree on that. Just imagine what it would be like if Hellie spent the summer somewhere else. Or Charlie."

"I don't want to go home," I said reluctantly. "But this

is the right time to go."

"Nobody's going to stop you, darling," Kate said. "When a woman needs to leave, she leaves." She must have been thinking of a woman arguing with Johnny von Dragondorf in some castle turret.

We finished our breakfast in silence. As I chewed my sausage, I imagined getting up from the table and going off to my room to pack. Most of the things they had stolen from our car at the start of summer were Primrose's and I didn't even want to touch them. The things I wanted to take with me had accumulated memories along the way. My diary, which was now battered and filled with notes. The knife from Kate. The printed programme from the bandits' Summer Shindig. The stick I'd saved after roasting my sausage on it over the campfire that first night, when I still thought I'd be free after a few days.

"Well, I guess I'll go and pack my things," I said. I already knew my stuff wouldn't even fill the Hello Kitty backpack. Packing would only take a few minutes.

"Go and pack," Wild Karl said in his commander's voice. "Five minutes to departure."

Everyone stood up in an orderly fashion. Kate began clearing the table while the others dashed off to their rooms to gather up their things.

"What's everyone doing?" I said.

"Well, of course Finland's most feared bandit van will

be taking you home," Wild Karl said. "That's what we agreed. Besides, I'm curious to see where you're from. And if Charlie starts school next Wednesday, this is our last chance to do some proper robbing."

"A little heist along the way, eh, Boss?" Hellie said as she came into the hall with her fully packed rucksack on her back. She even had her rolled-up sleeping mat tucked under the top flap, in case we needed to spend the night on the road. "Come on, just a little one."

On the way, we stopped one car where Hellie sniffed out some extras for her Barbie doll collection. She had sold all the original dolls that used to hang by their necks in the van's windows. Now she needed some replacements so the van wouldn't seem bare. Charlie got a real maths book – the same series we used at my school.

"What a pain," he said as he leafed through it. "We'll need to buy one after all. This one's no use. Somebody's done all the exercises in it."

I glanced through the book to look at the answers – the sums I checked were all correct.

"It's not a total waste," I said with a grin. "Hang on to it. Later you'll be happy you've got this one."

We marked the halfway point in our journey with a stop at our favourite cinema chain. I took them in for one last haul of sweets before they would have to make do with basic robbing again. The cinema foyer was unusually crowded. Summer holidaymakers had returned to the city. Teenagers were excited about the latest horror movie. Couples were there for a romantic comedy, and families with small children were going to see an animated film. I had gone in with Hellie and Golden Pete. They knew what everybody else wanted. On my list were toffee trucks, raspberry boats and old-fashioned peppermint sweets. The trucks and boats were for Hilda, who had finally found her ideal flavour combination after sampling different ones all summer. The striped pillow-shaped peppermints were the only ones that could help Kate figure out the ending to her novel. When she sucked on them, dressed in her woolly socks, she could close her eyes and know exactly what Johnny von Dragondorf should do. Would he fall in love and stay with the long-haired young woman or continue his adventures as a handsome, brooding vagabond? Even if Kate wasn't sure yet, the rest of us knew how the novel had to end. Of course Johnny would continue on his journey. How else could Angela Heartwell's next novel come about?

In one corner of the cinema foyer was a rack with some old DVDs on sale at bargain prices. I began looking through them and checked whether Hellie and Golden Pete were watching me. As usual, they were only interested in the pick 'n' mix. I was able to purchase a couple of

DVDs without them noticing.

Hellie grabbed a whole handful of bags. She opened one up, picked up one of the plastic containers that was full of liquorice bugs and started pouring them into the bag. An assistant standing nearby looked worried. "It's OK. We always take large portions," I reassured her.

Some children who had been looking at the DVDs stared at Hellie.

"What?" she said, imitating their big eyes. Then she flipped open the next two containers of sweets and, using both hands, started pouring wrapped liquorice and raspberry-flavoured chewy toffees into a single bag. An excellent blend for evenings, and one that gave you a sore jaw for two days afterwards.

Suddenly Golden Pete let out a gasp. He took two huge steps to the end of the pick 'n' mix aisle, then came to a stop and knelt down in front of one container.

"I've found you," he said. "You've tested my faith, innit. I started to doubt whether you even existed, but all along you've been waitin' for me right here."

Then he embraced the plastic container as if it was a long-lost friend. Parents began steering their children away from Golden Pete towards the tills.

"All right, you can have two kinds of sweets..." one mother said, distracted by the man who was stroking the lid of a container of sweets.

"I knew you'd be waitin' for me at the end of the road, if I just kept on believin'," Golden Pete mumbled. Then he planted a wet kiss on the lid.

The assistant let out a sound of disgust. "Ew, who's going to want those now?"

"We'll take the whole container," I said in a low voice.

"Hellie!" Golden Pete called out. "Come and look at this. A whole container of alien puke!"

A label on the lid of the container he was hugging said, "Place leftovers here. Container emptied every Friday."

We returned to the van with our purchases and woke up the others. Only Hilda was already awake, drumming her fingers on the steering wheel. She looked disappointed that we didn't need to make a fast getaway. I chucked a bag full of toffees to Wild Karl. He plunged his hand inside eagerly.

"Not many people come out of there with sweets," Wild Karl said, picking some toffee from his back teeth. "I paid attention, had time to people-watch when you were in there for so long."

"They've got ice cream as well," Charlie grumped.

"Don't worry, darling, we'll rob a kiosk somewhere and get you an ice cream," Kate said with a wink in my direction.

Then I said, "I've got a surprise for you all. But it takes some time to put together, so let's not leave just yet."

I asked Charlie and Golden Pete to give me a hand.

I opened the storage compartment under the rear seat and brought out a small portable TV and a DVD player, which were part of the previous week's robbing haul. Wild Karl had wanted to throw them out, but I assured him they would be useful. And they were, right here and now, as I had figured out a way to get an electricity supply into the van. I asked Charlie to set up the TV. It fitted perfectly on the luggage rack in back.

The TV was quite small. It was the kind you often see at car boot sales and in people's attics, now that everybody has flat screens.

"This is a DVD player," I explained as I secured it to the luggage rack. "And these are DVDs that contain movies, all with the right subject matter. *Robin Hood. Ronia the Robber's Daughter. Pirates of the Caribbean.*"

"What do we do with them?" Hellie asked. She clearly wanted to master the new technology ahead of the others.

"I'll explain once we've reached our destination," I said. "It's a sort of farewell gift. It will help to pass the time. It's meant for those long evenings when you're keeping watch somewhere. For winter days when you're snowed in and have nothing but time." I finished my adjustments. "All right, it's ready. Let's go," I said.

Hilda had been waiting for the signal. She hit the gas pedal and we headed out into the traffic, tyres squealing as usual.

As we ate sweets and squabbled in the van, I kept forgetting I was on my way home and soon wouldn't be with them any longer.

"Pete won the sweetie-swapping game this time," Hellie said. "It's no use playing any more. Nothing beats alien puke. You'd win with that anywhere in the world."

I looked out of the window. Suddenly I recognized the scenery we were passing. There was the hospital where we went when I broke my finger sledging.

"Turn left here," I said to Hilda. "Continue past the library and the school. That's where Drum Street starts. It leads to our place."

"Is that your school?" Charlie asked. I nodded.

"We're already nearly there," Wild Karl said in a sad voice. "Soon you'll be leaving us. How on earth will we cope without you?"

"We'll be fine," Kate said. "Don't listen to my brother. He's always talking nonsense."

The van turned into Drum Street. There were tall apartment blocks ahead.

"That second building," I said. "Stop here in the car park."

The van made a sharp turn and jolted to a stop. I opened the door and leaped out. I was standing in the car park, our car park. Now I could imagine how Hilda and Wild Karl felt to stand in front of their own home after such a long time away. I looked at Primrose's window. The curtains were shut. I knew she would be inside listening to music and talking on the phone. The curtains in my room were open. Anyone could look down here and see me summoning the courage to gather up my things and actually walk through the door and into the lift to my own home.

"You can still change your mind," Hellie said when I went back to the van. As I picked up my backpack, she spread out her arms. "Look, none of us would hold it against you if you got over there, then turned round and said, 'Naah'. We'd all understand. At any rate, we've had a nice day out."

"Will you be OK?" Kate asked.

"It's for the best," Hilda said. She didn't turn to me, just looked straight ahead through the windscreen. I could see she was crying.

"This is awful," Charlie said. "I thought it would be nice, but it's awful."

"At the start of summer I never thought I'd say this, but it's true: It's been real nice doin' heists with you," Golden Pete said politely. "It was like the big time, textbook-style. Us folks here in this van owe you a big debt of gratitude."

"Stay in touch," Hellie said. She handed me one of her customized Barbie dolls from the range she'd stolen just before the Summer Shindig – it turned out she hadn't sold them all. "You can private message me on the Bandit H forum. The code you need is tattooed on the doll's inner thigh."

She leaned down to get something. "Here, take these," she said brightly. "Good idea to practise so you're ready for when you join us again."

I didn't need to unfold the papers to know what they were. They were targets like Hellie used for knife-throwing. I definitely wouldn't be allowed to throw a knife at the wall at home, so I would need to figure something out. I put the targets in my rucksack and tried to think of how to say goodbye. I felt sad and a bit numb.

Charlie held up his maths book and nodded farewell. He was too sad to say anything.

"Have fun at school, Charlie," I said.

"Isn't anyone going to say it?" Wild Karl said with a sniffle. "Cowards! You've been trained better than that. All right, I'll say it. I'm the one who has to say everything, as the captain of this bunch. Don't leave, Maisie. This crew is so much better with you. Who will take notes and analyze the situation and all the rest…? None of us want you to go, even though we're pretending to be such big, tough bandits."

"Dad," Hellie said. "Don't."

Karl Robberson sniffled. Then they all sniffled, some more openly into tissues, others more like Hellie – looking out of the window, trying to seem brave.

Then I said, "My dear Robberson crew, I would like to

confirm that under the terms of our agreement, you will come back to steal me from this car park on the first day of June next year. We're all agreed on those details, right?"

"Yes," Hellie said, turning to look at me. Her face showed no sign of her previous emotions. "Agreed."

"Oh!" Wild Karl said, relieved. "Of course!" He held out his hand for Hilda to give him a tea towel. He used it to wipe his face and then blew his nose into it. I didn't want to see what he did with it afterwards. "That's an excellent plan."

"Karlito, when will you ever learn that everything involving Maisie will be a good plan?" Kate said.

"You'd better go, Maisie, otherwise we'll run out of tea towels," Wild Karl said.

"Just one more thing," I said. I took one of the DVDs down from the luggage rack. "You should probably start with *Robin Hood*. It'll make you laugh, guaranteed."

I took the DVD out of the case, put it in the DVD player and handed the user manual for the player to Hellie. I trusted she'd figure out what to do when the film was over.

"See you, everybody," I said. "I hope it's a short winter. I'll see you next June the first." Then I pressed the Play button and got out of the van.

EPILOGUE
which takes place during the walk
from the car park to the lift

This was the best summer ever. This was the summer I became a highway robber.

I learned how to eat breakfast straight from the pan next to a lake. I learned how cold it gets when you sleep outdoors.

I learned the best tricks for nicking things from cars and how to use a disguise for a heist in broad daylight.

I learned how to seem scary and how to come up with a signature crime. I will never be the same girl who only had choir and violin lessons to look forward to.

I can hardly wait for next summer.

Dear Reader,

Thank you for picking up my book, a story about a family of robbers who drive fast and act tough but don't care about money, only steal what they need (they love sweets!) and then by mistake pick up a girl, Maisie, who to everyone's surprise is ready to join the adventure.

I have always been inspired by Astrid Lindgren, by her stories and how she wrote *Pippi Longstocking* for her daughter. I wanted to write a story for my son, who loves speedy adventures and grand emotions. Although the book was written with my son in mind, for me it's important that the story is enjoyed by everyone. Books that appeal to all readers are much more interesting.

The world of the Robbersons is full of anarchy; they don't follow the rules. The robbers rev the engine of their battered van and speed off, they stop for a swim wherever they want, they steal sweets and run away from the police. I believe that books for children don't need to be so conventional; they should inspire readers to question the norms. For me this story is about freedom, about letting your hair down and heading where your nose leads you. A little mischief is not a bad thing.

This book was originally written in Finnish ten years ago and it has been translated into over twenty languages. I am thrilled that readers can finally enjoy this book in English!

Best wishes,

Siri Kolu, author

Dear Reader,

The bandits' world that Siri built was huge fun to re-create in English, especially the names! Some have stayed the same as in the original Finnish, but for names that convey a particular meaning I chose to create new equivalents in English – including for the Robbersons themselves. In Siri's original Finnish stories, they are the Rosvola family. *Rosvo* means 'bandit' or 'robber'. The ending -*la* occurs in many Finnish surnames, so although Rosvola is not a real Finnish surname, it looks as if it *could* be. I wanted to come up with a version that fulfilled the same criteria in English: a description of the family's occupation plus a common ending, combined to form a fake but plausible-sounding surname. That's how the Rosvolas became the Robbersons.

Like much of the world's best children's comedy, this book also contains details that readers of all ages will appreciate – such as Wild Karl's management style. The Robbersons live according to their own principles and traditions. Their attitude might prompt readers to reflect on their own lives, just as Maisie learns to adapt and see things from a new perspective.

There's a whole world of great stories out there. I'm glad I could play a part in bringing this fantastic book to you in English. I hope you enjoyed the adventures of Maisie and the Robberson clan!

Best wishes,

Ruth Urbom, translator

About the Author

SIRI KOLU studied in Helsinki and now lives with her family in Vantaa, Finland. She is an author, dramatist and writing mentor and is very active in Finnish literary circles. She's written sixteen books for children, of which *ME AND THE ROBBERSONS* is her breakthrough with a film of the book out and several theatre productions. It is one of the most widely known and translated middle grade novels from Finland, and Siri continues to receive invitations to tour from around the world. The book won the Finlandia Junior Prize, was included in the IBBY Honour List and won the Zilveren Griffel, which is the most important award a translated book can receive in the Netherlands. Kolu's stories combine the essence of Astrid Lindgren and Roald Dahl with explosive humour.

About the Translator

RUTH URBOM translates from Finnish, Swedish and German into English. She especially likes translating books that are fun to read! Other books she has translated from Finnish include *COW BELLE BEAUTY QUEEN* by Leena Parkkinen and *BICYCLING TO THE MOON* by Timo Parvela.